FORGOTTEN SECRETS

SECRETS OF THE HEART SERIES - BOOK 4

ELIZABETH ROSE

ROSESCRIBE MEDIA INC.

TO MY READERS

Secrets of the Heart is a series about the daughters of the bastard triplets from the *Legendary Bastards of the Crown* which is followed by *Seasons of Fortitude*. This series can be read as standalone books, but if you prefer to read them in chronological order, I have listed the series below.

Legendary Bastards of the Crown:
    Destiny's Kiss – Series Prequel
    Restless Sea Lord – Book 1
    Ruthless Knight – Book 2
    Reckless Highlander – Book 3

Seasons of Fortitude Series:
    Highland Spring – Book 1
    Summer's Reign – Book 2
    Autumn's Touch – Book 3
    Winter's Flame – Book 4

Secrets of the Heart Series:

Highland Secrets – Book 1
Seductive Secrets – Book 2
Rebellious Secrets – Book 3
Forgotten Secrets – Book 4

Enjoy!

Elizabeth Rose

PROLOGUE

ENGLAND, 1386

*D*eserted and overgrown, the secret garden stood forgotten and neglected being naught but a memory of the past.

Morag Douglas dismounted her horse and gently laid her hand on the old garden gate. Hesitant, yet anxious, she prepared to enter a place that she had always respected and admired. So many experiences had happened within these garden walls. Memories of her life were locked within, but would hopefully never be forgotten.

This had once been a place where Morag, her sister, Fia, and her cousins, Willow and Maira, came when they wanted to sneak away from the turmoil and trials of life. It was a place of solace to comfort their souls. It was also where the mysterious old woman, Imanie, who used to live here, had mentored the girls. But now, things had changed. Imanie was dead and everyone was gone. Everyone, that is, but Morag.

"Daughter. Let's make this a quick visit so we can get back to the castle to collect yer things and head back to Scotland." Reed Douglas, her father, who was one of the Legendary Bastard triplets of the late King Edward III, slid off his horse to follow her.

"Nay, Da." Morag held up a halting hand. "I must enter by myself."

"It's a garden, Fia. What's the difference if I'm there or no'?"

"Da! Ye called me Fia!" Morag crossed her arms over her chest and pouted, not liking the fact her own father had referred to her by her older sister's name. It was as if he couldn't remember her even though she was standing right next to him.

"Sorry, Morag, but ye ken what I meant. I guess I was just thinkin' about hurryin' back to Scotland to spend time with little Oletha. I'm so excited that Fia gave me my first grandchild."

"Aye, so she did." Morag's heart sank in her chest. It seemed she had lived in the shadow of her older sister, Fia, for as long as she could remember. Glancing down to the heart brooch pinned to her chest, she reached out and gently ran her fingers over the smooth surface. This was a pin that symbolized the members of the secret group of strong women started by the late Queen Philippa. Morag was not a chosen member of the Followers of the Secret Heart like her sister and cousins. Nay, she was naught but the forgotten daughter of a royal bastard triplet, not important or memorable enough for the queen to choose for this honorable position.

"If ye're goin' to pay one last visit to the secret garden then ye'd better hurry," instructed Reed. "I want to get back on the road as soon as possible. I'll wait here. Now go."

"Thank ye, Da," said Morag, pushing open the creaky gate and stepping onto the crumbled stone path that wove through the mysterious garden. She took a moment to scan her surroundings. This place had, at one time, seemed so magical and full of life. Tall, colorful flowers, thick bushes, unique trees, and even a variety of vegetables used to grow here. But now, with the girls' mentor gone, as well as it being so late in the year, the garden had died. Once a sanctuary, now it had been neglected and forgotten over time. Just like Morag.

She pondered this thought as she slowly made her way up the winding, overgrown path. The weather had turned for the worse lately, causing all the beautiful, colorful flowers and lush vegetation to dry up, turning brown and brittle.

Pulling her cloak tighter around her, Morag shivered, not sure if she shook from the cold or from the uneasy feeling that engulfed her as soon as she entered the garden. Focusing on the area up ahead, she walked directly over to Imanie's grave. The old woman lying beneath the cold earth had, at one time, mentored the other girls. Morag had wanted desperately to be included in this secret group. That is why Imanie had given up her own heart brooch to Morag, making her a member. The action meant the world to Morag at the time. However, now she wished the woman hadn't given the brooch to her at all.

Approaching the gravesite, Morag swept away the dead leaves with her foot and knelt on the half-frozen ground. A wooden cross that was made of sticks marked the final resting place of the mysterious and very wise woman.

"I miss ye, Imanie." Tears formed in Morag's eyes. Imanie

had been the only one who ever made Morag feel noticed and important. But the old woman had also told her that no one but the queen was supposed to appoint someone as a member of the secret group. Only once before had Imanie done this and, because of it, someone died. It was like a curse and something that never should have been tampered with in the first place.

"Ye shouldna have given this to me." Morag unclasped the heart brooch and held it out in her open palm as a regretful form of an offering. "I killed ye," she whispered, honestly believing that because of her greediness, wanting what her sister and cousins had, she had placed a curse on the old woman that took her life. Nay, it wasn't Imanie's bad heart that snuffed out her life, because Imanie had the purest heart of all. "I wish I could return this to ye and bring ye back to life."

Morag turned the brooch over in her palm, feeling her heart become very heavy. Hadn't her sister and cousins always teased her and accused her of being the cause of the death of their mentor? Morag had denied it but, deep in her heart, she couldn't help wondering if it were true. Now she was convinced that it was.

"Hurry up, Morag," called out her father from the gate. The wind picked up, scattering dried leaves around her. The eerie rustling sound felt like dead souls encircling her, taunting and scolding her for her mistake. It made her shiver. Although there was nothing but death in this garden, the sudden movement of the dried leaves made it seem as if they had a life of their own.

The sun disappeared, replaced by a threatening, dark sky. It seemed as if it were going to snow. Her father calling out to her again interrupted Morag's perusal of the heavy, dark clouds looming above her.

"Branton went ahead to the castle with the wagon to collect yer things," he told her. "Let's go, Morag."

"Just a minute, Da. I'm no' finished yet," she called back over her shoulder. The urgent need to leave this haunting place made her want to flee. Still, something caused her to stay. Her legs felt as heavy as lead as she knelt atop the grave. It was almost as if she were embedded into the ground. A part of her felt as if she belonged here. As she studied the gravesite, the thought of Imanie lying in the frigid earth made her spine stiffen.

Then, looking back to the brooch in her hand, she decided what she had to do. Her cousins and sister had accomplished outstanding things in secret using their unique skills. Because of their actions, it had changed the lives of others. It was what the Followers of the Secret Heart were expected to do.

Morag could never do anything like that. She wasn't able to use a sword like Maira, or to read people's actions like her sister, Fia. Neither was she any good at flirting or using the power of persuasion like her cousin, Willow. Nay, Morag didn't have any skill at all. The only thing she excelled at was gossiping. And that, she was sure, was not a trait to be admired.

"I dinna deserve this brooch and never did." Morag used a rock to dig into the hard earth, making a hole near the base of the grave marker. Then she brought the pin to her mouth and kissed it quickly before dropping it into the hole and covering it back up. "I have returned yer brooch, Imanie. Ye are the only one who should have ever worn it. Thank ye for noticin' me when no one else did. Because of ye, I started to believe that I could someday do wonderful things like the others. But I canna, and we both ken it. My sister is married now and has a baby. My cousins are married and pregnant. I will never marry and have bairns, because I am no' desirable to any man."

"That's not true, Morag. You should have a higher opinion of yourself."

Morag's eyes popped open wide, thinking at first that Imanie was speaking to her from the grave. Then she realized the faint woman's voice came from the porch of Imanie's cottage behind her. She jumped to her feet and turned to look, her jaw dropping open when she spied the wispy image of Imanie standing there, clutching her cloak around her tightly.

"Imanie," whispered Morag, feeling her heart beating like a drum. Her eyes flashed back to where she'd just buried the brooch, wondering if her wish had come true. Had her action somehow brought the woman back to life?

"Nay, I'm not Imanie," said the woman, stepping off the porch and coming toward her. "I am Imanie's sister, Mazelina."

Morag eyed the woman curiously. Beneath the old woman's hood, she had very similar features to Imanie. But instead of green and yellow eyes like the girls' late mentor, this woman's eyes were bright blue. She also stood a head span taller than Imanie.

"I didna ken Imanie had a sister." Morag's gaze fell to the heart brooch pinned on Mazelina's cloak and she gasped in surprise. "Ye're a member of the secret group as well."

"I am." The woman smiled and nodded. "Though I wasn't chosen, my sister declared me a member. I haven't seen her in years. And now that I've returned, I see it is too late." She pointed a long finger toward Imanie's grave. "Imanie is dead."

"Aye, she is," admitted Morag, wiping a tear from her eye with the back of her hand, still feeling responsible. "I'm sorry."

Mazelina held little expression at all. It was not at all how Morag thought she'd react.

"My sister will be missed," said the woman, keeping a stone-like face. Her words and voice were void of emotion of any kind. "How did it happen?"

"They say it was her heart." Morag's eyes traveled back to the ground where she had buried the brooch. Grief overtook her.

"You don't believe that's how she died, do you?"

"Nay, I dinna," Morag admitted. "I think she died because she gave me her heart brooch when I wasna worthy of bein' a member."

Mazelina walked over to Morag, studying the ground. Her hand caressed the heart brooch pinned to her cloak. "I understand. But you need to know that if my sister gave you her brooch, it was because she knew you would someday do something of extreme importance. Never belittle yourself, Morag. I'm sure that is what Imanie would tell you. Instead, have confidence that destiny has a plan for you just as it did for Fia, Willow, and Maira."

"Do ye really think so?" she asked, feeling a spark of hope ignite deep within her.

"I know so," answered the woman with no doubt at all resounding in her voice.

"Wait," said Morag, thinking something was a little odd. "If ye just arrived after bein' gone for years, how do ye ken me or Fia, Willow and Maira?"

"I don't know any of you," answered the woman, smiling at Morag.

"Did Imanie tell ye about us?"

"Nay. She didn't." Mazelina shook her head. "I heard you talking to Imanie."

"Oh, I see." Morag didn't believe she had been talking loud enough for the woman to hear her, but didn't want to call her a liar when they'd just met. "How did ye ken my name?"

"I heard your father calling you."

Morag supposed it could be true, but something in her nature made her remain suspicious. "Do ye have a skill as well?" she asked Mazelina curiously, wanting to know more.

"We all do, Morag. And you don't need to be leery of me."

Morag's head snapped up. How did she know? "What do ye mean?"

"Even if I hadn't heard you talking about your sister and cousins, I still would have known about them anyway."

"I dinna understand," said Morag. "How could ye? If ye havena seen Imanie in many years, and she did no' tell ye about us, then how do ye ken?"

"I have a special skill, my dear. I can hear the thoughts of others."

"Like readin' minds?" Morag asked excitedly. Then she narrowed her eyes and shook her head. "Nay. I dinna believe in such witchery." The idea intrigued her but frightened her at the same time.

"It's not witchery," answered Mazelina with a soft chuckle. "It's a special . . . skill."

"I still dinna believe it," she answered stubbornly. Her father had always taught her to only believe in what was real.

If something couldn't be explained, then there was no truth to it.

Mazelina looked over Morag's head toward the gate, narrowing her eyes as if she were concentrating on something. "Your father," she mumbled.

"My da?" Morag was still suspicious. "What about him?"

"He is thinking about coming in here in a few minutes to get you. He is also irritated that it is taking you so long."

"I'm sure ye heard him tellin' me to hurry." Morag raised her chin and crossed her arms over her chest. "That is no' mind readin'. That is common knowledge."

"Are you so sure? After all, I was in the house, so how would I know these things?"

Morag anxiously glanced over at the gate and then back to Mazelina. "I'm surprised my da hasna forgotten I am even here." Despair gnawed at her heart as she thought over and over again about the fact that her father had called her Fia. "No one seems to ever remember me." Anger mixed with grief and despair flowed through her like a raging river.

"They don't remember you? Is that really what you think?" asked the woman.

"I dinna think it, I ken it."

Mazelina surveyed Morag, nodding slowly. "If so, then do something that will get you noticed. Then you will never be forgotten."

"Like what?" Morag held her palms up and shrugged her shoulders, feeling hopeless. "I have no skills except for gossipin' and that is no' a skill at all. No one admires a waggin' tongue."

"Then turn your vice into a virtue," Mazelina told her with purpose. "Use your meddling for good instead of bad."

"Use gossip for guid instead of bad?" Morag pondered the thought. "How? That is no' possible."

"Isn't it?"

It seemed to Morag that instead of answering her questions, the woman only asked questions of her own. That irritated Morag.

"I've upset you," said the woman, as if she knew what Morag were thinking. Either way, Morag needed answers.

"Can ye teach me how to use my gossipin' for a guid purpose?" Morag asked, wanting to have a mentor of her own. The things Mazelina said sounded crazy but, at the same time, were like words of salvation to Morag's ears. Perhaps Mazelina could be the answer to Morag's problems, granting her deepest wishes as well.

"Mayhap I can help," said the old woman. "If you would like me to."

"Aye, I do," Morag answered anxiously.

Mazelina nodded once again. "All right then. In the spring, return to Castle Rothbury and come here to the secret garden to see me. But you cannot tell anyone about our encounter. This is the only way I will help you."

"Dinna tell anyone?" Morag was so excited that she wanted to shout it to the world.

"Not a soul," answered Mazelina. "Not your father, and not even your sister or your cousins."

"No one?" asked Morag once again, feeling the need welling in her chest to tell someone. If she had to keep it to herself she was sure she would explode.

"No one," repeated Mazelina in a stern voice. "If you tell a soul, I will not help you. Instead, I will leave you and you will never see me again."

"Nay," cried Morag, feeling a knot twisting in her stomach. This was something she wanted more than anything. But could she really keep it a secret? It would be torture not to tell her sister and cousins. Aye, it would be the hardest thing she ever did in her life. Still, she had no other choice but to keep it to herself.

"So, then, ye will be my mentor?" Morag's heart soared. This was what she'd always wanted. Now she would be included and feel like a real member of the secret group. "Ye'll guide me and teach me how to do great things, the way Imanie taught Fia, Willow, and Maira to do?"

"No one can teach anyone to do great things, Morag. That comes from inside here." Mazelina tapped her fingers against her chest.

"But I dinna ken how to do important things on my own."

"You need to have faith in yourself and it will happen in time, just like it did for the others."

"Can ye teach me how to have faith in myself – like ye said?"

"Are you willing to learn and also to change your ways? After all, your inability to keep a secret might be what's kept you from believing in yourself all this time. A wagging tongue can cause a lot of damage that, in some cases, can never be reversed."

Morag thought about all the times she had blurted out secrets that her sister or cousins didn't want anyone to know. Aye, she supposed she had caused trouble in the past from repeating things she knew or heard. But, perhaps, Mazelina could help her change.

Morag took a deep breath and released it slowly. She had to do this. This was an opportunity that she couldn't let pass her by. "I ken what ye mean and, aye, I would like to try to change."

"Trying and doing are not the same. The first steps in understanding yourself are to know what you want and not to let anything keep you from reaching your goal."

"Aye, I want it!" Morag exclaimed. "I want ye to mentor me so I can find my true talent and do important things like my sister and cousins. But why can I no' tell Fia, Willow, or Maira about ye? After all, they are Followers of the Secret Heart. I dinna think I should have to keep it a secret from them."

"We have a deal," Mazelina reminded her. "If you choose to honor it or not is up to you."

"Morag," came her father's shout from the opposite side of the garden. "Quit talkin' to yerself, and let's get goin' before it snows." Reed walked up behind her. His shoulder-length, red hair gently lifted around his shoulders in the breeze. His long, woolen cloak like an Englishman would wear was draped over his plaid – the markings of a true Scot.

Even though Reed and his brothers were born from English parents, they grew up in Scotland. Reed had always considered himself a Scot, like Ross Douglas, the man who raised him. Reed eventually married his Scottish sweetheart, Maggie Gordon. Morag's family lived in Scotland now while her cousins' families lived across the border in England.

Since childhood, Morag had been fostered by the Earl of Northumberland, along with her sister and cousins. But now, everyone had gone their separate ways. Her sister and cousins were married and even the earl had left, off fighting for the king.

Morag didn't want to be alone. And that is why they'd

returned to collect her belongings and head back to Scotland. There she would be reunited with her family once again.

"I'm no' talkin' to myself, Da. I'm talkin' to –" Morag stopped short when she remembered Mazelina's warning. Turning back, she was surprised to find that the woman was no longer there. Perhaps, she had headed back into the house or, mayhap, the stable. All for the better since her presence here was supposed to remain a secret.

After letting out a deep sigh, Morag bit her tongue, trying hard not to let the secret slip from her lips. "I'm ready to go now," she told her father instead.

Reed put his arm around her shoulders and escorted her toward the gate. "As soon as we collect yer things, we'll join up with Branton and be on our way back to Scotland where ye belong. Yer mathair, sister, and brathairs await us."

"Branton doesna need to come back to Scotland with us, Da," said Morag, talking about the boy of five and ten years who had been friends with Morag and the other girls since they moved to Rothbury to be the earl's wards.

"Aye, ye are right," her father agreed. "However, Branton will be makin' the trip with us at his insistence to help see to yer safety. Now that he's a squire to Maira's husband, Sir Jacob, he willna be able to stay away from Durham long. But he says he wants to protect ye even though I'm with ye." Reed chuckled. "There is no need for him at all, Morag, no' when ye've got me." Reed tapped the hilt of his sword to prove his point.

"Then why did ye allow him to join us?" asked Morag in confusion. She liked the lad but would rather have had time alone to spend with her father. Morag always longed for the attention from her father that he'd graciously given Fia.

"I needed someone to drive the cart," her father answered. "Besides, an extra sword is better than a servant who canna fight at all. Since we're crossin' over the border, it is always a guid idea to have more protection."

"I suppose ye're right," answered Morag as they got to the gate and mounted their steeds.

"Take one last look at yer precious secret garden," Reed told her. "This will be the last time ye ever see it."

"Perhaps it will, and mayhap it willna," said Morag, looking back over her shoulder, trying her hardest not to say a word about her plans. Excitement filled her to think about returning in the spring. Finally, she would have the chance to be mentored like the others. And with being the only one, Morag wouldn't have to share the attention. This is exactly what she had always longed for.

Perhaps, Mazelina was right in saying that destiny had plans for her after all. Morag wished for Imanie to come back to life and, in her place, her sister appeared. What were the odds of that happening? Whatever plans destiny had in store for her, Morag only hoped that she would never be forgotten again.

CHAPTER 1

ENGLAND, SPRING, 1387

*S*pring couldn't come fast enough as far as Morag was concerned. And although she loved being back home in Scotland with her family and Fia's new baby, all she'd been able to think about all winter long was returning to the secret garden. It had been excruciatingly hard to keep quiet for so long about Mazelina. Morag felt extremely excited and wanted more than anything to tell her sister. But what was even harder than keeping her secret was trying to think of an excuse to go back to England once winter was over.

She had been at her wit's end trying to come up with a story that would allow her to return. It wasn't going to be easy since her mother was thrilled to have her home after so many years. And her father swore he would never let his children live in England again, even if it was by order of a king.

Morag had just about given up hope of ever being mentored by Mazelina. Then, one day in spring, destiny poked its head out of the snow like a seedling pushing its way through a crack in the ground, searching for the sun. Aye, an opportunity arose that she never thought would happen for her. She was determined to use it to get back to England after all.

"Da! Mathair! Someone approaches," called out Morag's brother, Conall.

"They're bluidy Sassenachs," added his twin brother, Dugal, rushing up behind him. The boys were almost six and ten years of age now and already much taller than Morag. They were turning into men quickly and were no longer boys. Conall had red hair like their father and Dugal's hair was dark like their mother's. Both boys were slim but Morag noticed muscles forming in their arms from all the time they spent practicing with the sword.

"There's someone here?" asked Morag excitedly, handing baby Oletha back to Fia and rushing for the door. Her father got there first and stepped in front of her to block the exit.

"I'll take care of this," announced Reed in a low voice, sliding his sword out of the sheath. "If they're Sassenachs, it can only mean trouble."

"Faither, ye're a Sassenach, as well as yer brathairs and their wives," Morag reminded him, getting a nasty glare from him in return.

"Laddies, Morag, get away from the door," called out their mother. "Fia, take the bairn into the back room and hide until yer faither tells ye it is safe to come out."

"Aye, Mathair," said Fia, picking up the squalling babe. "I wish Alastair were here to protect us." Fia had been visiting her family with the baby while her husband, Laird Alastair MacPherson, had stayed with his clan in the Highlands.

"I wish Uncle Duff was here," said Conall, speaking of their mother's brother.

"Haud yer wheesht, all of ye," snapped Reed. "Ye make it sound like ye dinna think I can protect ye. Have ye forgotten who I am?"

"Nay, Da," said Dugal. Then the boys answered in unison and in a monotone as they rolled their eyes. "Ye are a Legendary Bastard of the Crown."

"Come on, lads," said Maggie, heading to the back room of the cottage.

"We ken how to fight," complained Dugal.

"We've got our own swords," added Conall. "Let's get those bluidy Sassenachs."

"Ye heard yer mathair, now go!" commanded Reed, sending the boys hurrying off after their mother. "Ye, too, Morag," said Reed, keeping his attention focused on the approaching traveling party.

Morag peeked around her father, sticking her head out the door. Two mounted English guards and a messenger approached the cottage. Another man traveled behind them atop a horse, but she couldn't see him well from her position behind her father's massive form. As the English came closer, Morag recognized the messenger boy as well as the crest on the horse's trappings.

"Da, that's Barnaby, Lord Beaufort's messenger," she told him anxiously.

"It is?" asked Reed, pushing her behind him in a protective manner. He squinted his eyes and held tightly to the hilt of his sword as the party rode closer.

"Aye, and if I'm no' mistaken, isna that Branton behind the

guards?" Morag poked her head under her father's arm this time to get a better look.

"Why in God's name would Lord Rothbury send them here?" mumbled Reed, reaching out and holding on to the doorframe to keep Morag from leaving the cottage.

"Let's find out!" Morag quickly ducked under her father's arm and ran out to greet the visitors.

"Morag, get back here!" shouted Reed, hurrying after her.

"Branton!" Morag waved a hand in the air as she hurried to meet with the travelers.

"Morag, how are you?" Branton slid off his horse and ran over to greet her. She felt so happy to see him that she threw her arms around his neck in a hug. "Where is Fia?" asked Branton, releasing her and looking toward the cottage. "I can't wait to see her and her cute little baby again."

"Fia?" Morag dropped her arms to her sides, feeling defeated. Branton looked right past her as if he didn't even know she was there.

"Fia is in the house with the rest of the family," Reed answered for her, joining them. "Go on in, Branton," he said with a nod of his head. The boy hurried off into the house more excited to see Fia and the baby than he was to see Morag. It didn't feel good to Morag at all. She was the one, along with her cousin, Maira, who had the closest relationship with the boy. Yet, no one would know it by the way he acted.

"Barnaby, why are ye here?" asked Morag, turning her attention to the messenger so her father wouldn't see the disappointment on her face.

"Aye," said Reed, still holding tightly to his sword. "What would cause ye to risk yer lives with a trip onto Scottish soil?"

"We come in peace, Douglas. You can put away the sword,"

stated one of the guards, lifting his hands to show he wasn't a threat and held no weapon.

"I'll no' put down the sword unless I feel like it," snapped Reed. "After all, ye are stinkin' Sassenachs and ye are on my land and uninvited."

"Faither, please," begged Morag as she spied one of the guards move his hand toward his sword. She had to interfere before a fight broke out. "It's all right, Da. I'm sure they mean us no trouble." She reached out and rested her hand on her father's forearm.

"That's right," said the messenger. "We are here at the request of Lady Rothbury to deliver a message." Barnaby reached down from atop his horse, handing Reed the missive.

"Did ye say, Lady Rothbury?" Reed reluctantly sheathed his sword, keeping his eyes on the guards' movements at all times. Then he took the parchment from the boy. "Dinna ye mean Earl Rothbury?"

"Nay, my lord," answered the boy with a quick shake of his head.

"I'm no' a laird," grumbled Reed, opening the missive and scanning it quickly.

Morag watched as her father's face clouded over. His mouth turned down in a frown.

"What is it, Da?" asked Morag in concern.

"Here. Read it for yerself." Reed handed the parchment to Morag and looked back at the house. "Conall, Dugal, come take care of the horses," Reed called out, causing Morag's brothers to run out of the cottage so quickly that Morag realized they had been waiting at the door. Then her father spoke to the guards. "Ye are welcome to come inside the house to rest for a spell. My wife, Maggie, will offer ye food and ale."

"Much obliged," said one of the guards as they dismounted their steeds.

Morag read the missive, feeling her heart skip a beat in surprise. "Nay!" she exclaimed, not wanting to believe what she read. "The earl has died!"

"What is it, Morag?" Fia rushed out of the cottage with her mother at her side. "What's wrong?"

Branton followed behind them carrying the baby, apparently so distracted by Fia and her daughter that he hadn't even told them the sad news.

"Lord Rothbury died fightin' for the king," said Morag, unable to believe that their guardian was gone. She felt a surge of grief wash through her.

"Nay!" shouted Fia, grabbing the parchment from Morag to see it. "It canna be true."

"It is," said Branton, bouncing the baby in his arms and making faces at the little girl until she smiled. "Since the earl has died without issue, the king said Castle Rothbury and all the earl's holdings are going to be given away."

"Given away?" asked Morag's mother. "I canna believe it."

"Why tell us?" sniffed Reed. "We are Scottish and have no interest in any castle or lands unless they are on this side of the border."

Branton continued to make faces at the baby as he explained everything to them. "Lady Rothbury is having a huge gathering at the castle. King Richard won't let her keep it since she is a woman and the earl had no heir. Since the earl died protecting Richard, he has allowed Lady Rothbury to help decide who will claim the earl's demesne."

"She wants us all to come for the feast," said Morag excitedly. "It said so in the missive. Da, mayhap ye'll get a castle like Uncle Rook and Uncle Rowen after all."

"If I own a castle someday, it'll be in Scotland, no' England," snapped Reed. He pulled the missive out of Fia's hand and shoved it back at the messenger. "As soon as the horses are rested and ye've had yer fill to eat, ye and yer guards can head right back to Rothbury. Tell the earl's wife thank ye but that we decline the invitation."

"Da, nay!" cried Morag, knowing this was her only chance to get back to England. "We were invited, and it is only proper that we go."

"Morag, I canna go," said Fia. "I need to get back to the Highlands. Alastair is waitin' for me. Plus, it is too dangerous of a trip for the bairn." She reached over and took her baby back from Branton.

"We want to go," shouted out Conall as the twins took the reins of the guards' horses.

"Aye, Da, we want to live in a castle," added Dugal.

"Be quiet," scolded their mother. "Yer faither has already made his decision and we'll respect it."

"Lads, ye are old enough now that ye'll stay here to be married this spring," Reed announced.

"Married? To who?" asked Conall.

"Whoever I choose for ye. I assure ye that the lassies will be Scottish."

"Then we're no' goin' to England?" whined Dugal.

"Nay, we'll stay right here in Scotland where we belong," Reed said in finality.

"But Da, there will be lots of single knights there," said Morag. "Mayhap I'll even find one to marry. After all, I am older than the twins, so I should marry before them. Then I can have a bairn like Fia and give ye a grandchild as well. Dinna ye want more grandchildren?"

"No daughter of mine is goin' to live in England, or marry a Sassenach," growled Reed. "So get that absurd idea out of yer head right now."

"Reed, the girls already lived in England for nearly ten years of their lives," Maggie reminded him.

"That was only because the king ordered it," growled Reed. "Morag, when I decide to betroth ye, it'll be to a Scot and no' a stinkin' Sassenach. Do ye hear me?"

"But I'm already well past marryin' age," Morag reminded him. "And Fia got to choose her husband, so I should, too." Morag had to get back to the secret garden and this was the only way to do it. She needed to convince her father to let her go. Morag crossed her arms over her chest and lifted her chin in the air defiantly, challenging Reed and waiting for his answer.

"Morag," gasped Fia because of the bold way Morag approached their father. "Ye were no' given that permission from the king like we were." Fia spoke about herself as well as their cousins, Willow and Maira.

"Fia, take the bairn back into the house before she catches cold," said Maggie, throwing a glance of sympathy in Morag's direction.

"Mathair, I really want to return to Rothbury," begged Morag. "Please convince Faither to let me go." If she were going to be mentored by Mazelina in secret, this was the only chance she would get. Morag had to get there without divulging the secret. It was eating her up not to be able to say a word about it, but she had kept her promise thus far.

"Reed, Lady Rothbury was the girls' guardian," Maggie

reminded him. "Morag is correct in sayin' we should show our respect for the loss of her husband. I think not only her, but all of us should go to Rothbury to support Lady Ernestine in her time of need."

"Nay." With a set jaw, Reed shook his head stubbornly. "There is no reason for our family to be there. There will be plenty of others to comfort her. Besides, ye ken that I never wanted the girls to live at Rothbury in the first place. Therefore, I dinna feel we owe anythin' to the late earl's wife."

"Reed Douglas, ye are as stubborn as an old goat!" Morag's mother crossed her arms in front of her chest as well. "If ye want everyone to ken that we were no' appreciative of what the earl did for our girls, then so be it. But I dinna agree with ye at all. Ye are lettin' yer hatred for yer late father cloud yer judgment."

"Nay, I'm no'," protested Reed. "Besides, Edward is dead and gone so what does it matter?"

"Ye act like ye hate the English, and that has to stop."

"But I do hate them," said Reed.

"Quit foolin' yerself." Maggie matched her husband, not afraid to stand up to him. "Just like Morag said, ye are really English. Just accept the fact and quit pretendin' to be a Scot."

Reed ran a hand through his hair. "I dinna care. I still dinna want to go."

"Then I'll just go," offered Morag. "I will represent our family so Lady Rothbury kens how appreciative we are for her guardianship. I'll also tell her that we are sorry about the earl's death."

"I dinna like it," mumbled Reed, looking at the ground.

"It's all right, Reed," said Maggie, taking Reed by the arm. "I will stay here with ye and the children. If Morag wants to go, let her. After all, Lady Rothbury sent her messenger with a missive all the way to Scotland."

"Not only a messenger, but two guards and me as well," said Branton, overhearing their conversation.

"Why are ye even with them?" asked Reed. "I thought ye were squire to Maira's husband now."

"I am," answered Branton with a smile. "But Lord Jacob let me come along with the traveling party because I missed Fia and Morag and wanted to see them."

"Umph," grunted Reed.

"Can I go back to Rothbury with them? Please, Da?" begged Morag, pouting like she used to do as a child, hoping to change her father's mind. "I'll only be there until the festival is over. Mayhap a few months and then I'll return home."

"A few months?" Reed made a face. "It shouldna take that long to find a new lord of the castle."

"But the festivities dinna start for over a fortnight yet," Morag reminded him. "Didna ye read that in the missive?"

"Let her go, Reed," said Maggie. "It seems to mean a lot to her."

"Aye, it does," agreed Morag. "Besides, I'm sure Willow and Maira and their husbands will probably be there, too."

"Oh, I doubt it," said Branton, earning him a stomp on his toes from Morag as well as a dirty look. He jumped up and down holding his foot.

"Will any of you be returning with us or not?" asked one of the guards walking out of the house munching on an apple. "I'd hate to think we made the journey all the way here for naught."

"Ye havena, because I'll be returnin' with ye." Morag

looked up to her father, pleading with him once again. "Can I go, Faither? Please?"

Reed looked at her and then over to Maggie. With both Morag and her mother staring at him, Morag knew it wouldn't be long before he crumbled.

"Och, all right," he finally agreed, swiping a hand through the air. "Morag, ye can go to Rothbury, but only until the end of the festivities."

"Thank ye, Da." Morag threw herself into her father's arms and gave him a big hug. "Ye willna regret it."

"I already do. And I warn ye, Daughter, stay away from the laddies. If I find out ye've married a Sassenach behind my back, I swear, it'll never be forgotten."

"Never be forgotten?" Morag pondered the thought, and a smile slowly spread across her face. Hadn't Mazelina told her that if she didn't want to be forgotten that she should do something to be noticed? Well, now, here was an idea! Morag now knew exactly what she had to do as soon as she arrived at Rothbury. She would find herself an English knight and get married.

CHAPTER 2

CASTLE ROTHBURY

*M*orag was surprised to see the scattering of tents already pitched outside the curtain wall when they rode up to the gate of Castle Rothbury a few days later.

"Why are all these tents here?" she asked Branton.

"Those are the tents of the knights wishing to win the favors of Lady Rothbury. They are hoping they'll have a chance to claim Lord Rothbury's castle and holdings as their own," explained Branton.

"But I thought the decision wouldna be made for nearly a fortnight yet."

"That's right. However, it will take some time for all of the men to have an audience with the lady of the castle. I am sure they will start early. There is a lot at stake and only the first fifty knights to register will be eligible as agreed upon between King Richard and Lady Rothbury."

"Only fifty? Why?"

"The king wants to narrow it down because he is a busy man. He has let the earl's widow send invitations to her husband's most trusted friends and allies. However, if some of them decline, then anyone can take their spots. It looks like there are a lot of knights who don't want to miss out on this wonderful opportunity."

"That's right," grunted one of the guards. "Earl Rothbury had one of the largest castles in all of England as well as some of the most prestigious holdings. He was favored by the late King Edward."

"How is Lady Rothbury goin' to decide which knight will take it all?" asked Morag. "And will she make the decision alone?"

"Nay." Barnaby spoke up this time. "She will make her choice and the king will have to agree. She is going to have private audiences with the knights, talk to them, and test their skills on the practice field to determine who would best be granted the holdings. Then she'll recommend a few men to the king and he is the one who will decide who gets it all."

"My, this is even bigger than I thought." Morag looked around the grounds as they rode over the drawbridge. Squires busily staked their lords' colorful tents and tended to the horses, while servants busied themselves making cook fires and preparing food. Everyone bustled about busily, but still they watched as she rode into the castle. "I wish my faither would join in the competition. He deserves a castle, although he would never live in England. Were my Uncles Rook and Rowen sent a missive as well?"

"They were," said Barnaby. "However, they both turned down the invitation."

"Why would they do that?" asked Morag, appalled at hearing this.

"I think they were being modest," Branton told her. "Even Willow and Maira's husbands were invited to compete but said they were happy with what they had."

"That's absurd," spat Morag. "I think they all declined only because they ken Richard has never liked them. Either that, or love must have addled their brains. What about Alastair? Fia's husband? Was he invited, too?"

"He's a Scot," growled one of the guards.

"So is my da, but he was sent a missive," Morag pointed out.

"That's only because your sister and you were once wards of the earl, and your father was the Black Prince's bastard cousin," explained the second guard. "We all have suffered much because of the death of the Black Prince as well as by the death of King Edward."

"Ye make it sound as if ye dinna like Richard bein' king." Morag noticed a bit of animosity and wanted to find out more.

"He's not the man his father or grandfather were," mumbled another of the guards.

"Haud yer wheesht," spat Morag, telling them to be quiet. "That is yer sovereign ye are talkin' about, no matter what ye think of him. I am a Scot and yet I still respect yer English king."

"You are right, my lady. Guards, back to your posts," said one of the men and they all dispersed.

Morag smiled inwardly being called my lady. She liked the title even if she wasn't sure it was real since her father wasn't a knight and she was only a bastard cousin of the king. "I miss

Lord Beaufort." Morag thought about the man who had been her guardian for many years. "The earl was a kind man. His wife is even nicer."

"You should try to convince your father and uncles to come to Rothbury," said Branton. "I don't know any knight who wouldn't want Castle Rothbury and the earl's lands as his own."

"Do ye think so?" asked Morag, looking around the crowded courtyard. Castle Rothbury was, indeed, one of the largest and most majestic castles in all of England. She had lived here while growing up and gotten lost within the mazes of corridors until she got used to her new surroundings. "Just seein' all these knights and squires, it might be too late by the time they even get my missive askin' them to come."

"Then you can sign them up while you're waiting for their reply," commented Barnaby.

"That's right," added Branton. "I think I'll sign up Lord Jacob while I'm here. Then I'll send him a missive to change his mind about declining the offer."

"Perhaps I should," said Morag, not really thinking of castles, lands, or competitions right now. All she had on her mind was getting back to the secret garden to see Mazelina so she could start her training.

SIR BEDIVERE HAMILTON OF GAUNT rode through the gates of Castle Rothbury feeling extremely unsettled. The last time he was here was about a year ago and, at the time, his cover had almost been blown wide open. Being here wasn't a good feeling at all.

Lady Willow had discovered his secret profession and it hadn't sat well with him. She had said she'd keep his secret, but what if she hadn't? The missive he received from Lady Rothbury asking him to apply for the late earl's holdings came at the same time as his orders for his next job. He was to wait here until further notice. Being suspicious of everyone, he couldn't help thinking this all might very well be naught but a ploy to expose him as an assassin.

"Why the hell did Whitmore choose this place to give me my next assignment?" he grumbled to himself, thinking about the king's advisor, a man he hated more than anyone he had ever met in his life. He scanned his surroundings, always aware of what went on around him at all times. He had to be this way. It was the nature of the job. Usually, a contact met with him, giving him the missive that would tell him the name of his next kill.

However, his orders were usually given in private. This place was much too busy for anyone to be discreet. The contact would meet him here soon, but it wasn't to his liking. Still, he had no other choice. And now that he was here, he would have to pretend he was interested in acquiring the late earl's holdings. If he didn't, it would be too conspicuous that he had come for a different purpose altogether.

It had been a long two years, but one more assignment is all he had left. After that, he would be finished with this ungodly job forever.

Being an assassin of the king had turned Bedivere into a very ruthless, bitter, cold-blooded man who no longer had emotions. He had accepted the job in trade to save his life, bringing him out of the dungeon of Whitmore Castle where he had been imprisoned. Bedivere's life had been spared that day, but in return he had promised to take out a dozen men who were conspiring against the king. Only when he had killed twelve men who were plotting the king's demise would he and the other captives be set free.

"Lord Bedivere, hello," called out a female from behind him.

He twisted in the saddle, surprised to see one of the daughters of the Legendary Bastards of the Crown standing there. It was the gossipy one. He couldn't remember her name, nor did he care. All that mattered to him was that her cousin, Willow, hadn't told her about his occupation.

"Hello . . . Fia," he said, hoping that was the right name.

"It's Morag," she scowled, her eyebrows dipping down in frustration. "Fia is my sister."

"I'm sorry that I forgot your name, Morag."

"It figures," she mumbled under her breath, raising her chin as if she felt insulted. "Everyone forgets me."

"Are your cousins here as well?" Looking over her head, he scanned the courtyard.

"Nay. They are all married now and at their new homes with their husbands."

"Aye. So, does your cousin, Lady Willow, ever . . . talk about me?" He slid off the horse and stood across from her now.

"If ye are wonderin' if she wishes she married ye, she doesna." The girl had the audacity to roll her eyes as if the suggestion were absurd. "She never says a word about ye, and neither does she care."

"Good," he said, releasing a breath he'd been holding. It seemed Willow hadn't revealed his secret after all.

"Guid?" asked the girl, cocking her head curiously. Her

eyes bored into him and he felt as if she could see clear through to his very soul. That is, if he had a soul anymore, which he sincerely doubted. He was sure all assassins went straight to hell. Either way, he had better watch his step around this one before she spun a tale about him and spread it throughout the castle.

"What I mean is . . . that's good that she is happy with her new husband," he corrected himself. "I'm surprised to see you here, Maira."

"Morag," she said with a sniff. "How many times do I have to tell ye?"

"Morag. Sorry. I thought you would have gone back to Scotland to be with your sister."

"I was back in Scotland but now I'm here. And I ken why ye are here, Sir Bedivere, and I must say it disgusts me."

"You do?" Bedivere's heart sped up. Mayhap he had been mistaken and Willow had talked after all. The last thing he needed was this one to know the truth. All of Christendom would know what he did for a living if she got wind of it.

"Aye. Ye want the late earl's castle and lands for yerself, but ye dinna need them. I hear ye are one of the richest knights in all of England." She had a smug look on her face as if she felt proud of herself for knowing this. It didn't impress him since it was a rumor he had started himself.

"Aye," he said, building on what she thought she knew about him. "I am here to compete for the late earl's castle and lands. Why wouldn't I?"

"Because, ye are rich and dinna need it. Leave it for someone like my da who doesna have half of what men like ye have."

"Men like me?" He perused her from the sides of his eyes.

"Now, now, Morag," he said, stressing her name so as not to roil her again by mistaking her for her sister or her cousin. "I am not as rich as you think."

When he had started the rumors about himself, he hoped by saying he was wealthy that it would form people's opinions about him. No one would ever question his actions if they respected him for being rich. If only they knew he hadn't more than a bag of coins, his armor and weapons, a horse, and a change of clothes to his name. He didn't work for money. He worked for trade. Thankfully, he'd been supplied with the tools he needed for his profession, but that was as far as it went. He didn't even have a place to lay his head. Nay, Bedivere didn't have a castle. He didn't even have a home. Traveling from job to job, he bided his time at functions such as this one, not having anywhere else to go. Everything Bedivere once had was gone now, including his pride and self-respect.

"Well, how rich are ye?" she asked in her meddlesome way. She took a step closer. "What did ye say was the name of yer castle, Sir Bedivere? And where exactly is it?"

He couldn't answer this, and neither did he want to.

"Is yer castle in Gaunt? How big is it? How many men are under yer command?"

The girl was persistent with her questions and also very nosey. He didn't want to back himself into a corner so he decided to change the conversation.

"If you'll excuse me, Lady Maira," he said purposely using the wrong name so she'd forget her questions and pout about that instead. "I need to pitch my tent before nightfall."

"I think ye ken my real name and are just callin' me Maira to anger me." She crossed her arms over her chest and stared a hole through him. She was a sharp one, even though one wouldn't know it by just looking at her. "Ye are tryin' to change the conversation as well."

"Me?" he asked, feigning amusement. His hand went to the hilt of his sword – a nervous reaction he always used when he felt cornered. "If I may say so, Lady Morag, you have very beautiful brown eyes. And your hair glows with a golden aura, almost like an angel."

"I dinna believe ye," she said, not buying his compliments at all. "And where is yer squire? I've never heard of a knight pitchin' his own tent."

"I only say what I mean, my lady. And my squire is . . . away on an errand at the moment." Bedivere cringed inwardly. Why had he just said that? He didn't have a squire and now Morag would constantly be looking for one. He had to be more careful with his words. What was the matter with him?

He reached out and took her hand in his. True, he had made it a habit to flatter women when they started breaking down the walls he'd built around him to protect his secrets. Just like the way he did to Morag's cousin, Willow. He'd actually even tried to marry the girl! Now, he didn't know what he had been thinking. What had started as a game ended way too quickly, but he was thankful. Willow turning down his proposal of marriage was a good thing. Bedivere didn't want to marry. He was a loner, and would stay that way until the day he died. No more would he be controlled like a poppet because of his ties to his family. Besides, if a woman ever knew his secret, she would never want to be his wife and he couldn't blame her. His life was ruined now, and there was no way to regain that part of his soul that died the day he'd started being an assassin.

"What are ye doin'?" she asked when he brought her fingers to his mouth and kissed the back of her hand.

"It is proper of a knight to greet a lady in this manner."

"An English lady, mayhap. But in case ye didna notice, I am a Scot."

He noticed all right. How could he miss her thick Scottish burr or her bright strawberry-blond tresses that hung down to her waist? She also wore the plaid of a Scot instead of an Englishwoman's gown. A long-sleeved white tunic was covered by her short bodice that laced down the front. Her skirt was made of a dark green woolen plaid, and she had a sporran, or small bag, tied to her waist.

"Aye, and so you are a Scottish lady and a very beautiful one at that," he complimented her, finding it natural to say these words to get him what he needed.

"Ye are callin' me bonnie?" Her eyes narrowed as if she didn't believe him.

"Aye, you are beautiful," he told her, scanning the courtyard as he spoke, trying to find his contact.

"Ye are no' even lookin' at me," spat Morag.

His eyes darted back to hers. "I find myself so mesmerized by your beauty that I have to look away."

"Am I bonnier than my cousins, Willow and Maira?" she asked, surprising him by her bold question. Normally by now, he'd have a woman eating out of his hand and blushing from his words. "And how about my sister, Fia? Am I bonnier than her as well?" Morag continued.

"My lady?" he asked, not knowing how to answer. He never expected her to say this.

"Tell me, Sir Bedivere. Do ye say this to every lassie ye meet? Because if it is naught but a line that ye are feedin' me, then ye dinna need to waste yer breath. I, Sir Knight, canna be fooled by the likes of ye."

Shocked at the way Morag was hammering him with her accusations, Bedivere dropped her hand and stood upright. He had to remedy this awkward situation before it got further out of hand.

"Are you calling me a liar?" he asked, just to roil her.

"Are ye one?" she boldly answered in return. Then she stepped forward and pushed her face closer to his. Her lush lips were set firm and all he could do was stare at them since they looked so inviting. His eyes traveled upward, from the cute little dimple in her chin to the high cheekbones and the graceful but mysterious curve of her brows. His gaze stopped when he met her big, beautiful, brown eyes. For the first time, he actually studied her face and realized that while the words sprang from his mouth in a rehearsed reaction, he hadn't taken the time to drink in her true beauty.

"You think I'm a liar?" he asked, reaching out and lifting her chin with two fingers. Her bottom lip called to him in a seductive pout. Without meaning to, he cupped her cheek in a gentle caress, reveling in the feel of her soft skin. Aye, she truly was beautiful, and he was a fool for never noticing this before now. "Mayhap this will prove that I only say what I mean." He leaned forward and boldly placed his lips against hers. Having had a weak moment, he only meant to shake her up so she'd stop asking personal questions. But before he knew it, he was going back for a second helping. The girl's lips were soft and supple but she stood there like a dead fish, not knowing what to do. Still, he found her interesting and he liked it. The wench desperately needed to be kissed by a man and, by God, that was exactly what he wanted to do to her, over and over again.

The only thing that kept him from going back a third time was the sting of Morag's palm slapping him across the cheek.

"My lady," he said in surprise, stepping away from her holding his hand to his face. She had one hell of an arm. "I – I'm sorry. I got carried away proving to you that I meant what I said. I beg your forgiveness." Women didn't usually react this way to his advances. He should have known she'd be different since her cousin, Willow, had acted in much the same manner.

"Humph," she said, crossing her arms over her chest again in a silent gesture of pushing him out of her personal space. "I suppose I forgive ye, but dinna let it happen again or I'll have to tell my da." Her face lowered and she hugged herself tighter.

"Nay, don't do that," he said with a chuckle. "I have enough problems of my own and don't need a Legendary Bastard of the Crown hunting me down." The late King Edward's bastard triplets were to be feared. They were a force to be reckoned with and, at one time, were known as the Demon Thief, directing three different armies to raid their own father. Nay, he never wanted them coming after him, that's for sure. "I'll be on my way now," he said, trying to get away from Morag. If he stayed a minute longer, he'd want to kiss her again and that would only bring about trouble. What was the matter with him? He normally wasn't infatuated with the ladies. Then again, none of them he'd ever known were like Morag. She seemed to be a loner and wild at heart, curious and afraid of nothing. In a way, she reminded him of himself.

He turned and started away, but stopped abruptly when she called out to him.

37

"Sir Bedivere." Her voice sounded meek and breathy. Had his kiss done that to her?

"Aye, my lady?" He slowly turned around to face her.

"What is yer answer?"

"My answer?" He pushed back a stray hair from his face. "Answer to what?"

"Am I the bonniest one or is it my sister or perhaps one of my cousins?"

His eyes raked down her body as she hugged her arms around her tightly. She sent mixed signals and this confused him. She seemed so fierce and bold but, at the same time, unsure of herself. He didn't know what to make of it. Morag's cheeks blushed with a rosy hue. And when their eyes met next, her gaze quickly dropped to the ground. This made her seem shy. But she'd also slapped him hard which made her a feisty wench.

She continued to hug herself so tightly that it would take a pry bar to get her to drop her shield of protection. Aye, Morag Douglas was a very complicated girl. Being pretty to a fault, but with a tongue that wagged like a flag, he didn't know if he should trust her, fear her, or hate her. One minute she kissed him and the next she pushed him away. Oh, why did he have to contend with this right now? He had other worries on his mind and really didn't need the distraction.

"I'll tell you the answer to that, my lady, when you learn how to kiss a man properly," he replied. "After all, even a virgin like you should have some idea what to do while in a man's arms."

"What?" she asked. Her eyes blinked twice in a row. Her hug of protection loosened and her hands balled into fists, moving to rest on her hips. "What do ye mean, I dinna ken how to kiss?" Her face held the look of being insulted and her words dripped with venom. "And how do ye ken that I am a virgin?"

Well, he'd guessed correctly about that part. And in his experience, the girls who were virgins were always the most trouble. He had to say or do something that would repel her enough so she never wanted to be near him or ask him personal questions again.

"Forgive me for being so blunt but you kiss like a dead fish, my lady. And by the way you had your arms clutched around you so tightly, I can guarantee that it was not only your first kiss but also the first time a man has ever touched you. Now, if you'll excuse me, I have a tent to pitch."

CHAPTER 3

*M*orag stood in shock with her mouth wide open, not sure how to respond to Sir Bedivere's insults. It was a desirable thing to be a virgin, but no one liked to hear that they kissed like a dead fish! She had been thinking how romantic his kiss was, and how alive she felt by the tingle that ran through her. Silly of her to believe he might have felt the same way. Men like Sir Bedivere Hamilton were probably used to whores, she decided. Aye, that must be it. He most likely had never had a woman with royalty in her blood. He was most likely covering up his own insecurities by trying to point out hers.

"Did I just see Sir Bedivere kiss you?" asked Branton, walking up with the reins of a horse in his hands. He looked over his shoulder as he spoke.

"What if he did?" asked Morag, not wanting to admit she had acted so wantonly.

"Isn't he the one who wanted to marry your cousin, Willow?"

"Aye, I suppose he is," she answered nonchalantly, biting at a hangnail on her finger.

"That's right. He's the one who Willow said she didn't like. Didn't he try to get her into his bed before he even asked her to marry him?"

"Branton, there is no need to gossip!"

"Think, Morag. You remember. After the competition to choose brides and after Willow turned him down, he had her alone in his chamber. It almost caused a scandal. The father of the girl he was supposed to marry wouldn't let his daughter be married to the scoundrel after all."

"Branton, that is enough!" snapped Morag. "I dinna want to hear another word about it." She now found herself attracted to Bedivere and his brash remark of her not knowing how to kiss made her want to try it again.

"Morag?" Branton looked at her oddly. "You are the one who is always the first to spread gossip. What is the matter with you that you are telling me to be quiet?"

"Mayhap I've changed," she told him, feeling the need to jump into the conversation but yet she fought to stay quiet.

"Morag," called out Lady Ernestine Beaufort, the earl's late wife from the other side of the courtyard. She was thankful to be interrupted because if Branton kept up with this, she was going to join in and talk about Bedivere behind his back as well.

"Lady Ernestine!" Morag hurried over to the woman who had been her guardian for the past eight years. Branton followed on her heels.

"My dear, sweet child." Ernestine held out her arms and Morag rushed over to give her a hug. "I am so happy you are here." The woman wasn't any taller than Morag. She was a round, plump lady who could barely get her arms around Morag to hug her. Tears formed in the woman's eyes.

"Lady Ernestine, I bring condolences from my family on the death of the earl. He will be missed by everyone. He was a guid man," Morag told her.

"Aye, he was," said Ernestine, pulling back and dabbing a tear from her eye with a square of cloth. "Where is your family, Morag?"

"They didna come," she hated to admit. "It was too hard for Fia to travel with the bairn and all."

"I understand. But what about your father? Where is he?" Ernestine looked around the courtyard. "Don't tell me he's not here either. Didn't he get my invitation?"

"Oh, he got it," interrupted Branton. "I was there, so I know. He said he didn't want to come to Rothbury."

"Didn't want to come to Rothbury?" The countess' face clouded over and her smile turned into a frown. "Why not?"

"Branton," Morag grumbled, throwing him a daggered look. "Shouldna ye be headin' back to Durham Castle now that ye've escorted me to Rothbury?"

"I suppose so," said Branton. "I'll just sign up Sir Jacob to be considered for the earldom before I leave."

"Oh, don't go," begged the countess. "I do enjoy having you here, Branton. You lived here so long that you are almost like the son I never had."

"He is a squire now to Lord Jacob, my cousin Maira's husband," Morag informed her. "He needs to get back to Lord Jacob's side."

"Aye, but only to tell Lord Jacob I've put his name on the list. Then I'll be back along with him," Branton remarked.

"Nonsense, I'll send a messenger to tell him so you can stay here with Morag," insisted Lady Ernestine. "I feel so lonely now that the girls have all left and my husband passed on, so I would like you to stay. I'm sure another week or two without you isn't going to ruin Sir Jacob."

"Nay, that's no' necessary," Morag blurted out, not wanting Branton to stay. He had seen her kiss Sir Bedivere and would most likely tell everyone about it. Not that it bothered her that much, but he was also used to gossiping with her and it was going to be hard to stop if he was constantly whispering in her ear.

"I thank you, Lady Ernestine, and will take you up on the offer." Branton smiled widely, making Morag groan inwardly.

"Was that Sir Bedivere I saw talking with you, Morag?" The woman glanced across the courtyard to where Bedivere was now conversing with a guard.

"Aye," she answered, feeling the blush rise to her cheeks. "He left to stake his tent. It seems he is here as well as everyone else to compete for the earl's castle and lands."

"He also kissed Morag," Branton was sure to mention.

"Branton, haud yer wheesht," scolded Morag. "Ye have a waggin' tongue."

"Me?" Branton slapped his hands against his chest. "Everyone knows you are the gossip, Morag."

"Tent? Nay, he won't stay in a tent," said Lady Ernestine, ignoring the part about the kiss, most likely to help Morag save face. She looked over the heads of those in the courtyard to see Bedivere. "Branton, do go and tell Sir Bedivere that he is one of my most respected guests. Let him know I'll have a chamber prepared for him in the castle anon that he'll use during his stay at Rothbury."

"Aye, my lady," said Branton, bowing and taking off at a run.

"Nay, that's no' necessary," said Morag, feeling her heart beating faster. She wasn't sure she wanted the man inside the castle. What if he cornered her in his room the way he did to Willow? What would she do then? The man scared her but excited her at the same time. It had her very confused.

Lady Ernestine looked at Morag with a sly smile. "He is a handsome man, Morag. And even though your cousin had eyes for someone else, I can see you two belong together."

"Nay, I dinna think so." Once again, she felt the color rise to her cheeks. She wrapped her arms around her and looked to the ground, not able to meet Lady Ernestine's gaze.

"Branton said Sir Bedivere kissed you."

"It wasna like that. No' really. It was just a . . . friendly kiss."

"Morag, stop being so modest." Ernestine put her arm around Morag's shoulders, guiding her as they headed to the keep. "Your sister and cousins are all married now and, as your former guardian, I am going to make sure you find a husband before I leave Rothbury. I want to make sure you are well taken care of and I believe Sir Bedivere can do that."

"Ye do?"

"Aye. I hear he is rich, and we can all see he is handsome. He also seems to be very chivalric around the ladies."

"I – I suppose so."

"I remember from the previous competitions that he is well trained in weaponry as well. You will never have to worry about your safety around him, because I am sure he will protect you."

"Do ye really think so, Lady Ernestine?"

"I do. Sir Bedivere, I'm sure, would never harm you. He'd protect you with his life."

"But I'm no' sure Sir Bedivere is lookin' for a wife."

"Of course he is, or did you forget? He was here not long ago competing for the hand of a lady in marriage. To my knowledge, he still isn't married. It is a shame it didn't work out for him. He seems to have so much to offer."

"Aye," said Morag, contemplating the thought. "I suppose he does. How well do ye ken him?"

"Me?" Lady Ernestine's free hand went to her chest. "Well, of course I don't know him well, but I'm sure my husband did."

"Where is his castle, Lady Ernestine?"

"His castle?" The woman stopped walking and blinked twice. "Now that you mention it, I don't know. I just supposed it was somewhere in Gaunt, but I don't recall the name or location of it. Why don't you ask him?"

"I did, but he didna answer."

"He's probably being modest, Morag." Lady Ernestine smiled again. "Men like him don't like to talk about themselves. He is a true and loyal knight. Someone you can trust."

"Thank ye," said Morag, glancing back at Bedivere as he spoke to Branton. He looked up and nodded at Lady Ernestine. When Morag was sure he was heading over to thank her for the offer of the chamber, she decided it was time for her to leave.

"Pardon me, Lady Ernestine, but I think I'll go for a relaxin' ride."

"Oh, don't go outside the castle gates without an escort," warned the woman. "There are too many people outside the castle walls and it could be dangerous."

"I'll be fine," she said, trying to get away, but the woman was persistent.

"I'm sure Branton will go with you." Lady Ernestine waved him over as well.

"Nay, it's no' necessary." Morag wanted to sneak off to the secret garden and the last person she wanted along was Branton.

"Don't be silly. Branton can protect you, now that he's a squire. That's what squire's do."

Morag let out a deep sigh, seeing that she was never going to be able to sneak off alone to the secret garden again.

CHAPTER 4

"*B*ranton, go back to the castle," Morag called over her shoulder as she rode toward the secret garden with Branton following right on her tail on a steed of his own.

"Lady Ernestine told me to escort you on your ride to protect you and that is what I'm going to do," he answered stubbornly.

"But I dinna want ye here."

"Why not?" he asked.

"I want to be alone."

"You are sneaking off to the secret garden, aren't you? Why? No one is there anymore so there is no reason to go."

"It's none of yer business what I do, so stop askin' so many questions."

"Are you going to visit the grave of Imanie?"

"Aye. That's what I'm goin' to do and I want to be alone. So ye'll have to wait for me outside the gate." She rode up to the garden gate and stopped.

"Wait outside the gate? Whatever for?"

"I like to be alone when I visit Imanie."

"I won't bother you. You won't even know I'm there."

"Nay. I plan to be here a long time," she told him. "So ye might as well just turn around and head back to the castle. I'll meet ye there."

"I'm sorry but I can't do that," said Branton, dismounting. "I'm here to protect you. If you don't want me around, I'll wait for you in the cottage. I could use a nap." He stretched his arms over his head and yawned.

Morag panicked. She couldn't let Branton into the secret garden and certainly not inside the house or he would see that someone was living there. She had to keep him from seeing Mazelina or she wouldn't get mentored after all.

"Branton, I willna tell ye again. This is a secret garden, meant only for members of the Followers of the Secret Heart."

"What does it matter? You're the only one left now." Branton yawned again. "Besides, it's not even a secret anymore."

"It matters to me. Now, I command ye to stay outside the garden gate until I return."

"Oh, all right." Branton tethered his horse and sat down with his back up against a tree and closed his eyes. "I'll get a few minutes of shut eye, but don't take too long. I nccd to hurry back to the castle to add Sir Jacob's name to the list of contenders before it is filled. You should add your father and uncles' names to the list as well."

"I will. As soon as we return, I'll do just that."

As soon as she was convinced that Branton wasn't going to follow her, she slipped inside the secret garden, leaving her horse with the boy. After closing the gate behind her, she scanned the garden quickly.

"Mazelina?" she whispered, heading up the path to the

cottage. A cool spring wind blew and she lifted the hood of her cloak over her head, holding it close for warmth. "Mazelina, I'm here just like ye told me." Looking down, she spied Imanie's grave. While the rest of the garden was still covered with dead flowers and dried up weeds and fallen leaves, the grass atop Imanie's grave was bright and green. "Odd," she said, not giving it much thought before she hurried up the steps and barged into the cottage.

"I'm here, Mazelina," she called out. "I'm here to be mentored."

The inside of the house was dark since it was such a dreary day. She found a jar candle on a table next to the door and quickly lit it. "Mazelina?" she called out once more, thinking the woman might be sleeping and not have heard her. But when she held up the candle to see the room, her heart dropped in her chest. The bed hadn't been slept in and there was still dust covering the rickety furniture. She slowly lowered her hood, taking a good look around. She didn't see anything belonging to Mazelina and there was no evidence that anyone had been here since the last time she visited in the winter. Sadness filled her being as she realized that Mazelina hadn't waited for her. Perhaps, the woman had thought she wasn't coming and went back to wherever she lived. Now, Morag would have no chance of being mentored in the way the woman promised.

She turned to leave, startled, and screamed when she saw someone standing in the doorway.

"Branton! Ye fool. Ye almost gave me a heart attack. I thought I told ye to stay outside the garden."

"I intended to," he said. "But the wind blew open the gate and I swore I saw someone in the garden that wasn't you."

"Ye did?" Hope filled her being. "Was it a woman?"

"A woman?" Branton looked confused. "Why would you think that?"

"Oh, I dinna ken. I just wondered." She bit her lip, almost spilling Mazelina's secret.

"I don't know since they were covered by a hooded cape. Perhaps it was a woman, but the person was tall so mayhap it was a man."

"A man?" Suddenly, Morag became frightened and moved closer to Branton. "Who could it have been?" she asked.

"I don't know. When I entered the garden, the person seemed to disappear."

Morag quickly blew out the candle, not wanting to be there any longer. She felt an odd chill run up her spine like the last time she was here. Something wasn't right and she found herself thankful now that she had Branton with her for protection.

"Let's get back to the castle at once," she said, heading out the door of the cottage.

"But I thought you wanted to visit Imanie's grave."

"Later," was all she said, hurrying to her horse with Branton on her heels. She took one last look over her shoulder as she left the garden, wondering if something had happened to Mazelina or if, perhaps, she was in hiding. Was it Mazelina that Branton saw in the garden or perhaps another intruder? The thought frightened her. Quickly mounting her horse, she rode like the wind back to the castle, wondering if she'd made a mistake in coming to the secret garden or even coming to Rothbury as well.

* * *

BEDIVERE SAT in front of the fire in the hearth in his chamber, polishing his array of weapons. He bided his time, waiting to be contacted. He used a soft rag against the side of his best sword, seeing his reflection in the metal. Around his face were the colors of glowing red and orange from the flames. It made him look like the devil, and he felt like it, too.

He thought of the innocent Morag and the way she had all but melted in his embrace. Didn't the fool girl realize how dangerous he was? Of course she didn't. If she had, she would have done more than just slap him. She was too curious for her own good and too pretty for a woman who was naught but a wagging tongue. Loose tongues in his profession were a liability. Everything he did had to be in secret. He didn't even know who his contact would be since the person changed every time, just to keep from being caught.

He would have to stay far away from Morag because he couldn't risk her finding out why he was here or what he was about to do. Protecting the king was admirable, but not in the way he was asked to do it. He would much rather duel with an armed man face to face instead of slitting a man's throat from behind. But he'd only been doing as instructed, even if it didn't feel right. His victims never had a chance to defend themselves.

He stopped polishing the blade to run his fingers over the notches carved into the hilt. Eleven notches stood for eleven kills. One more to go and he could leave his tarnished past behind him. One more job and the person he loved would be free from an imprisonment she didn't deserve. Even still, he would never be free from the mark on his soul for who he was and the things he did. This bothered him immensely.

Anxiety coursed through him, causing him to stand up and

pace the floor. He thought his emotions had died through the years but, lately, they seemed to be coming back to life. He now felt turmoil within him before finding out his next kill. Like the darkness of the night, he lived imprisoned by his past and knew he would find no happiness in this lifetime, nor did he deserve it.

A knock at the door caused him to stand upright, his heart skipping a beat. It was late and most everyone had already gone to sleep for the night. It must be his contact. But just in case, he had to hide the evidence of his actions.

"Just a moment," he called out, quickly scooping up his weapons and wrapping them in a blanket to hide them. Hurrying over to the door, he pulled a dagger from his weapon belt, holding it steady as he stood to the side, reaching over and flinging open the door.

To his surprise, it wasn't his contact, but rather the meddlesome girl and her sidekick, the young boy he saw in the courtyard earlier.

"What do you want?" he growled.

She looked at him oddly, most likely expecting him to be standing at the door and not off to the side, half-hidden.

"Sir Bedivere, is that any way to greet a lady?" sniffed Morag. Her gaze fell to his hand and her eyes opened wide. "Why are ye grippin' yer dagger?" She took a step back, closer to the boy.

"Stand back, Morag," said the boy, pushing her behind him and drawing his sword. "I'll protect you."

"Branton, I dinna want trouble," she told him.

"Mayhap not, but it looks like he does." The boy was ready for a fight.

Bedivere groaned inwardly. Could he ever get a break? He

was tired and weary and all he wanted was one good night's sleep. That was something he hadn't had in years now.

"Oh, excuse me," he said, faking a laugh and pushing his dagger back through his belt. "I didn't mean to frighten you. I was polishing my dagger when I heard the knock, that's all."

"Oh," said Morag, eyeing him up as if she almost believed him.

"Was there something you wanted, Lady Morag? After all, it is late for a woman to be coming to my door." He scanned the hallway, watching for anyone who might be his contact.

"Well, that is why I brought Branton with me," she told him. "I dinna want to be seen as a strumpet, knockin' at yer door at all hours of the night."

"Then why are you here?" he asked, wanting her gone.

"I couldna sleep after what ye said about me. I had to talk to ye about it."

"Egads, are you serious?" Bedivere ran a weary hand through his hair.

"You said she kissed like a dead fish," said Branton, replacing his sword into the sheath.

"Really." He looked from one of them to the other. "Because of that, you saw fit to come knocking at my door in the dead of the night?"

"I willna have a man accuse me of somethin' that isna true," whined the girl.

"If you are looking for an apology, I'm sorry, but you won't get it. Now, go on to bed where you belong." He started to close the door in her face but she stepped in front of Branton and her hand shot out to stop it.

"Listen, I don't know what you want, but can't this wait until the morning?" he asked her.

"This willna take but a moment," she told him, reaching out and pulling him to her, kissing him deep and hard.

So much in shock was he that he didn't know how to react. She went from standing lifeless while he kissed her to kissing him so passionately that it set his loins afire. And when he thought she was going to pull away, she kissed him once more, this time, slipping her tongue into his mouth. All worries fled his mind and his manhood hardened at her seductive actions.

Then she stepped back and raised her chin, the tip of her tongue darting out to lick her lips, causing him to squirm since he was now very randy.

"I dare ye to tell me I kiss like a dead fish now."

"Nay," he said, shaking his head, not sure how to respond. "That kissing was more like . . . a Winchester Goose."

"A goose?" She crinkled her nose, apparently having no idea he meant a whore. That is, not until Branton leaned over and whispered in her ear. She listened and her eyes grew large and her jaw dropped. "How dare ye say that!" Her hand shot out to slap him but, this time, he was expecting it. He clasped her wrist in his fingers, pulling her closer and talking in a low voice.

"If you come to my room again at night, do so without your bodyguard because I am not fond of being watched when I bed a woman."

She pulled out of his hold and her arms clasped around her tightly as she once again hid behind Branton.

"I think it's time we go, Morag," said the boy.

"I agree," he answered, seeing someone in his peripheral vision heading to his room. "Percival," he muttered under his breath, shocked to see his younger brother at the castle.

"Who's that?" asked Morag as Percival stopped in the shadows.

"No one," he said. "Now go."

"Oh, it's yer squire," said Morag, waving a hand in the air. "Hello, I am Lady Morag. What is yer name?"

Bedivere squeezed his eyes closed and bit the inside of his cheek. Damn. Why did Morag have to be here? Now, he was going to have to address her question or run the risk of looking suspicious.

"Aye, it's my squire, Percival," said Bedivere, motioning with his head for his brother to come out of the shadows.

"Hello," said Percival, giving Bedivere a nasty glare for calling him his squire.

"I'm glad they told you that I'm staying in the castle instead of in a tent." He reached out and yanked his brother into the room. "Goodnight," he said to Morag, slamming the door in her face.

"Squire?" asked Percival, pushing out of Bedivere's grip. "Get your hands off of me, Brother."

"Shhh," he said, putting a finger to his lips. He waited a moment and then opened the door a crack and peered up and down the corridor. When he was sure Morag had left, he closed the door and bolted it. "I'm sorry about that, Percival, but I couldn't take the chance. The girl has a wagging tongue and is much too inquisitive for her own good."

"Oh. I understand," said Percival, collapsing atop the bed and falling back. "I just want this all to be over."

"You and me both. What are you doing here?" Bedivere went back and uncovered his weapons and continued to polish them.

"I was sent here by Whitmore."

"What?" Bedivere's head snapped up. "What the hell does that mean? I'm waiting for my contact."

Percival sat up on the bed and dug something out of his pouch and held it out. "I know. I am your contact."

"You?" Bedivere's blood boiled. "What the hell is Whitmore doing? I don't want you involved. It's much too dangerous."

"Not as dangerous as being locked behind bars in Whitmore's dungeon. Here, take it," said Percival, waving it in the air. "I don't want to even touch this bloody thing."

"Percival, I don't know what games they are playing but I don't like this. None of my family is supposed to be involved." He snatched the missive from Percival's hand.

"Read your orders," said Percival, yawning and laying back on the bed again. "Then go off and do your nasty deed to free Mother from the dungeon. And in the morning, I'll be on my way back to join the rest of our family."

"Nay, you can't leave until I do now that Lady Morag thinks you're my squire."

"What?" Percival sat upright with a snap. "Don't tell me I'm to play the role of your squire now. I won't do it."

Breaking the wax seal with his thumbnail, Bedivere scanned the missive, silently reading the name of his next mark. He froze, his heart almost stopping. "Nay! This can't be. There must be some mistake."

"There's no mistake, Brother. They told me to deliver the missive and that you'd know what to do."

"I can see why they sent you now," said Bedivere, pacing back and forth madder than hell. "Because if anyone else delivered this to me, I would have killed the messenger where he stood."

"What is it?" asked Percival, getting off the bed and coming to see Bedivere's orders. Looking over his shoulder, Percival gripped his brother's forearm tightly.

"Those bastards," spat Percival.

"That's right," growled Bedivere, throwing the missive into the fire to destroy the evidence. "It's not one kill to free Mother, but three now. It's a suicide mission and certainly nothing I want to do."

"I know, Brother, but you have no choice. You have to do it."

"Mayhap so, Percival. And you know I'd give my own life to free Mother. But tell me, how in the name of the devil am I supposed to take out all three of the Legendary Bastards of the Crown and live to see Mother again afterwards?"

CHAPTER 5

*N*ot able to sleep, Morag snuck to the stable just before dawn, feeling the need to go to the secret garden by herself to check on Mazelina. Still frightened, she hesitated to leave without an escort, but it was something she had to do. She promised the old woman she'd keep their secret, but with Branton tagging along, it was never going to happen.

Nervously, she gripped the hilt of the dagger hanging on her belt, her only means of protection. She had contemplated taking a bow and arrows or perhaps a sword with her, but decided against it. She didn't know how to use either. Besides, they would only slow her down if she were being chased and had to flee quickly.

Being quiet so as not to wake the stable boy, she saddled her horse and silently rode out of the stable. Since the drawbridge was up and the gate still closed from last night for protection, she had to sneak out the postern gate the way she and her sister and cousins used to do whenever they went to the garden in secret.

It wasn't easy to sneak past all the tents camped out front. But since the postern gate was at the back of the castle, she was sure she remained unnoticed. As she rode away, making her way to the secret garden, her hood fell down and her unbound hair blew behind her in the breeze.

* * *

HAVING HAD the worst night's sleep of his life, Bedivere made his way to the window and threw open the shutter for a breath of fresh air. Mayhap, this would help to clear his muddled mind.

Looking out from his window, he could see the back of the castle and the lands around it in the moonlight. Dawn was almost here and faint rays of sun lit up the horizon in a soft, orange hue. He took a breath and released it slowly, trying to center himself and push aside his emotions. He'd learned not to let his work bother him, but this last job was one that unsettled him deeply.

How the hell was he going to kill off the bastard triplets? It was a fool's mission and one that was sure to take his life trying. Plus, it didn't sit right with him having to kill off Morag's father and uncles. He felt something for the girl, although he wasn't sure what. This kill seemed too close to home.

Looking out at the horizon, he couldn't stop thinking about Morag and that kiss. How bold and daring was she to come to his room at night to prove his assumption of her was wrong. He saw sadness and loneliness within her eyes and recognized it as something that often haunted him as well.

Aye, she was a lot like him, and that only made him want to protect her.

"Damn," he said, running a hand through his tangled hair in thought. All he wanted to do was to protect the girl. But what she needed was to be protected from men like him.

He was about to close the shutter when he spotted a rider leaving the castle at a fast pace down the road. Long, blond hair blew in the breeze as the person headed for the woods. "Morag," he said, standing up straight, wondering where she was going unescorted and so early in the morning.

"What is it, Brother?" asked Percival from the bed.

"It's nothing," he said, closing the shutter and trying to block out the girl from his thoughts. Part of him wanted to follow Morag, but yet another part of him wanted to forget all about her at the same time. Now that he had his orders, he didn't want to think about Morag in a romantic way. Killing the bastard triplets was a secret he'd never be able to tell her, and neither would he ever want her to know about the heinous deed. If Morag ever did find out, she would hate him for eternity, and he couldn't blame her. His stomach twisted and his head swarmed in confusion. Bedivere already hated himself for what he was about to do. Still, he had no other choice. If he were going to save the last of his family, his mother, from the horrible dungeon, he would have to follow his orders and push aside any feelings he had for the girl.

MORAG ENTERED the secret garden just as the sun began to rise. With the reins of her horse in one hand and her dagger clutched in the other, she cautiously made her way toward Imanie's cottage.

"Mazelina?" she called out in a shaky voice. "Mazelina, I am here. It's me, Morag. I have returned to be mentored by ye just as we've agreed."

She tied up the horse and made her way into the cottage. Not seeing the woman anywhere, her heart sank and she turned to leave. As she made her way down the stairs, she saw something move in the stable. Gripping the hilt of her dagger, she picked up a rock in her other hand and made her way over to investigate.

When she entered the stable, she saw Mazelina at the opposite side of the stall.

"Mazelina! Thank God, I've found ye." She ran over to give the old woman a hug, but was stopped by her raised hand.

"There is no need for that," said Mazelina. "I do not hug anyone." Once again, there was no emotion in her voice.

"I'm sorry," said Morag, dropping the rock at her feet and pushing the dagger into the sheath at her waist. "When I didna see ye here yesterday and Branton said he saw a stranger in the garden, I was afeared that somethin' happened to ye."

"Fear is what holds us back from accomplishing great feats," said the woman, nodding to a wooden bench inside the stable. "Sit, Morag. It is time for your first lesson."

"Oh, guid," she said excitedly, plopping down on the bench. It was an old, rotten bench and it broke under her weight. Morag landed on the ground in the dirty, stale straw. "Help me up," she said, reaching out a hand, but Mazelina did nothing.

"If you can't even help yourself off the ground, how do you expect to help others?"

"What do ye mean?" Morag got to her feet and brushed the dirt and straw off her skirt.

"You have a lot of fears, Morag. That is something your sister and cousins did not have."

"Nay, I dinna fear anythin'."

"Be honest with yourself." The woman gave her a knowing look. "Remember, I can see into your mind."

"I guess there's no use in hidin' it then. Aye, I do fear some things."

"Tell me about them." Morag noticed that Mazelina always stood, but Morag decided to sit on a stool she found.

"I fear that I'll be forgotten and that I'll never get married or have bairns."

"Go on." The woman nodded.

"That's all."

"Is it?"

There she went again, answering questions with more questions of her own.

"I dinna ken what ye want me to say."

"I see something troubling you. Something that has to do with Sir Bedivere. Tell me about it."

Morag felt embarrassed and was hesitant to bring up her kissing episodes with Bedivere to anyone. "Well, if ye can see into my mind, then ye already ken what ye want me to tell ye. Therefore, I dinna see any reason to say it." She stood up and wrapped her arms around herself, staring at the ground.

"Your sister, Fia, would look at your body actions right now and see that you are lying as well as trying to close yourself off from the rest of the world. That is not the way to protect yourself."

Morag let out a deep sigh. It was no use trying to keep anything from her. "Oh, all right. I'll tell ye. I kissed Sir Bedivere and I liked it."

"And?"

"Stop answerin' me with more questions."

"And?" Mazelina asked again.

"And it scared me. There, I said it. Are ye happy now?"

"Are you happy?"

"Mazelina, I am here to learn from ye how to use my gossipin' in a positive way. Ye havena taught me a thing."

"Haven't I?"

"Stop it!" she cried, stamping her foot. "I want to be mentored the way Imanie taught Fia, Willow, and Maira. Teach me somethin' that I can use to make a difference, to do somethin' important in my life."

"I am not Imanie and I'll not have you commanding me to do anything."

"Ye're right. I'm sorry." Morag decided she'd better watch her step or Mazelina might decide not to mentor her after all.

"In order to learn anything, you will need to know yourself first."

"Ken myself?" Morag made a face. "I hope ye dinna mean in a . . . sexual way."

"Is that all you can think of? Kissing and making love?"

"Well, I admit, it has been on my mind a lot ever since my sister had a baby and my cousins married. I am eight and ten years of age and still a virgin with no husband. When will it be my turn?"

"When do you want to marry?"

"As soon as I can."

"What about loving a man? Does that matter to you?"

"Mazelina, most girls are married at a much younger age than me as part of an alliance. I dinna think lovin' a man really matters, do ye?"

"Is that what you truly believe?"

Morag felt flustered, and also very confused. She'd come here to learn a skill from the old woman and, instead, she got nothing but silly games and lots of questions.

"I think ye should tell me what to do and who to marry."

"I think you need to be a willing student if you are going to learn anything. Do not tell me what to do."

"I'm sorry," she said for a second time, disappointed that this wasn't going the way she thought it would.

"If loving the man you are to marry truly doesn't matter to you, then why don't you marry Sir Bedivere?"

Morag's heart skipped a beat. "Do ye think I should? Do ye think he'd want me?"

"Do you want him?"

"I – I dinna ken. I suppose so."

"Do you even know the man?"

"What is there to ken? I hear he is rich and that he is good with weapons and would be able to protect me."

"Mayhap so, but then again, how do you know what you hear is true? And do you want to marry an Englishman rather than a Scot the way your father wants you to?"

Morag thought about it for a moment, considering the consequences. "My faither doesna care what I want so I will do whatever I please. And I ken these things about Sir Bedivere are true because Lady Ernestine told me so."

"Well, who told her?"

"I – I am no' sure. Does it matter?"

"Your first lesson, Morag, is to listen to your inner instincts and not just accept everything you hear as the truth."

"But if everyone kens this, it must be true."

"Isn't that how gossip gets started?"

"I am no' sure."

"When you tell others what you hear, how do you know that the things you've learned are the truth and not just speculation?"

Morag stood up and leaned her elbows on the gate of the stall. She had never been asked this before and didn't know how to answer. "I suppose I dinna ken for sure."

"Then, once again, find out answers for yourself and turn a deaf ear to things that might be naught but idle gossip."

"So, I shouldna believe what I hear from others?"

"Can you trust the sources from which you are hearing these things?"

"Mazelina, my head is spinnin'. I am so confused. I didna expect ye to ask me so many questions." The old woman's behavior truly shook Morag's nerves. She had never expected her mentoring to be so hard. She didn't understand it.

"Isn't it exasperating when someone asks so many questions?" The old woman actually smiled when she said it. That made Morag realize she was making a reference to her and Morag didn't like it.

"I think I'd better get back to the castle before Branton realizes I'm gone and he comes lookin' for me." She hurriedly got to her feet, no longer wanting to be there.

"Will you be back?" asked the old woman.

Morag stopped at the stable door feeling dizzy from all the confusion in her head. Part of her no longer wanted to return.

But she knew if she didn't, she would never be able to earn her position in the group. That, she decided, was something she wanted more than anything, no matter how hard it was to attain. "Aye," she said with a sigh. "I'll be back. But when I return, will ye teach me somethin' I can use next time?"

"Haven't I taught you something already?"

Feeling exasperated by another question, Morag pushed a lock of her long hair behind her ear and shook her head. "Perhaps I need to return to the castle to think about this for a while."

Morag left Mazelina and the secret garden, wishing her mentoring had been something physical like Maira's training in fighting. Or, mayhap, even fun, like Willow's flirting with men to get them to do what she wanted. Right now, she would even welcome training on being able to read people's actions like Fia was able to do. Mayhap then Morag would understand the strange, old woman who seemed to have no emotions, asked a lot of questions, and who didn't want to be hugged at all.

Was Morag really being mentored to be a true member of the Followers of the Secret Heart? And would she, in the end, do something important or life changing like the other girls had? She wanted to believe she would, but it didn't seem probable or even possible at this point.

She rode back to the castle feeling let down and very shaken. Mayhap, she was never meant to be a true member of this secret group after all.

CHAPTER 6

"*I* don't like this," said Bedivere, pacing back and forth in his solar. His brother sat at a small table breaking off a piece of bread from a loaf he'd brought from the kitchen. A decanter of wine and two goblets graced the table as well.

"I don't like it either," complained Percival, chewing on a crust of bread. "I want a good meal and some entertainment, not stale bread and sour wine. We were invited to sit at the dais with Lady Ernestine, so I don't know why we're holed up in this stuffy room eating like peasants."

"We'll go down to the great hall in time, but not yet. First, I need you to help me decide what to do."

"What do you mean?" Percival shoved another chunk of bread into his mouth and chewed while he talked.

"Tell me again. What did the king's advisor tell you when he gave you my orders to deliver?"

"Lord John Whitmore was adamant that you had to follow the orders completely and that Mother wouldn't be set free until he was satisfied that you stopped this attempt on the king's life."

"Dammit, Percival, why is our family in this position?" Bedivere clenched his jaw, feeling trapped.

"I think you know that answer." Percival took a swig of wine to wash down the bread, making a face that told Bedivere the wine wasn't to his liking. "If father hadn't ruined things for us, we'd be living in a manor house in the country and I'd be married by now."

"I still don't believe that Father was organizing an attempt on King Richard's life. It wasn't like him."

"He often disagreed with the king. Plus, Father did have a bad temper." Percival poured Bedivere a goblet of wine and handed it to him. "Did you want any bread?" There was only a small piece left since Percival had eaten most of it.

"Nay, I'm not hungry." Bedivere took the goblet and sat down across from his brother. "It's been two years now, and I can't live this way anymore, Brother."

"None of us can," agreed Percival. "It was no joy being in Whitmore's dungeon, and it is far from accommodating with the ten of us all crammed into the small cottage made of wattle and daub. If Father hadn't done us in, we'd be living in a castle by now where we truly belong."

"Aye, I have often thought of that, too." Bedivere released a deep breath and took a swig of wine. "How are the others? Are they faring well?"

"As best as can be expected," stated Percival, licking the wine from his lips and thumping his goblet down on the table.

"Tell me about them, Percival. I want to hear about my family. It's been such a long time since I've seen them."

After their father was sent to the gallows for his betrayal to the king, Lord Whitmore advised King Richard to imprison and put Bedivere and the rest of his family to death as well. However, they were kept in the dungeons of Whitmore Castle in Staffordshire instead of anywhere near the king. The castle belonged to the lord's advisor, as well as the land and the cottage where Bedivere's family now resided. Only his mother was still imprisoned, as the rest of the family members were released one by one every time Bedivere killed off someone who had plotted to kill the king. Two years and eleven bodies later, and Bedivere was so close to having his entire family released. Once his mother was set free, he planned on taking her, his siblings, aunt and uncle to Scotland to live. Even though his father's death and Bedivere's family imprisonment had been kept a secret, it was only a matter of time before the word got out and the Hamilton family name would be sullied forever.

"If you came to visit once in the past two years, you'd know how they fared," sneered Percival.

Guilt ate away at Bedivere because his brother was right. Still, he couldn't bring himself to visit his family because of who he'd become. "It's not that I don't care. You know I do."

"Of course." Percival didn't believe him.

"I can't bear to see them living this way." Bedivere closed his eyes as he spoke. "And worst of all, I can't let my siblings look up to me like a hero after all the lives I've taken."

"Let them be the judge of that."

"Tell me. How are they, Percival?" Bedivere needed assurance that his family was all right.

"Well, Sarah and Avelina became sick during their stay in

the dungeon, and so did the twins, Averey and Luther. Uncle Theobald's sight is worsening and Aunt Joan says he's lost his mind."

"Oh no," said Bedivere, hearing about his siblings as well as his aunt and uncle. "What about Rhoslyn, Claire, and Elizabeth?" he asked, speaking of the eldest sisters. Bedivere was the first-born sibling, now four and twenty years old. He was followed by Percival who was two years younger. Then came their sisters followed by the twins who were only seven years of age. It made Bedivere furious that Lord Whitmore hadn't even balked at the idea of imprisoning children.

"The eldest of our sisters have taken over the duties and even gone to work at the castle to bring in food so we don't starve. I was there as the falconer's assistant until I was sent here to give you your last orders."

"I despise Father for putting us in this position," snarled Bedivere. "If he hadn't gotten cocky, he'd still be alive and I wouldn't have to clean up his mess."

"His mess? We don't even know if Father was really guilty of treason."

"And neither do we know that he wasn't," stated Bedivere. "All I know is that after Mother is released, my family will never suffer again. I will make sure of it!"

"Then you'll have to kill the bastards." Percival's eyes met Bedivere's and they shared a moment of silence, the air thick between them. "Do you think you can do it, Brother?"

"I don't want to do it, but I will take any action required to save Mother from that hellhole. I will take her away from the misery and suffering of losing her husband and seeing her children treated so poorly. I promise, she will never have to suffer again."

"Then you'd better think of a way to get the bastards here and fast. Are they coming for the competition for the earl's castle and lands?"

"I don't know," said Bedivere, taking another swig of wine. He banged the goblet down on the table and jumped up. "But I know someone who can get them here, and I will see to it that it happens."

* * *

"Where have you been, Lady Morag? I was worried about you." Branton met Morag in the stable, his arms crossed over his chest and a stern expression on his face. "You know you are not supposed to leave the castle unescorted. It's dangerous."

"I wasna gone long and there was no trouble so ye needna worry." Morag dismounted and opened her cloak. "Besides, as ye see, I had my dagger for protection."

"You're not Maira, Morag. You don't even know how to use a blade."

"Nay, I'm no' my cousin, and I'll warn ye no' to compare me to her again."

"You don't need to get snippy. I'm just trying to protect you."

"I dinna need yer protection."

"Then how about my protection?" asked a deep voice from behind her. Morag turned to see Sir Bedivere and his squire standing in the door to the stable.

"Sir Bedivere." Morag already felt the blush staining her cheeks just at his presence. "I didna ken ye were there."

"Pardon me for interrupting, my lady, but I couldn't help overhearing that you are in need of a bodyguard."

"Nay, she's not. She's got me." Branton stood taller and rested his hand on the hilt of his sword attached to his waist.

"Branton, dinna ye have to get back to Durham?" asked Morag through gritted teeth. "After all, ye are supposed to be Sir Jacob's squire now."

"Nay, it's all right. You know as well as me that Lady Ernestine sent a missive to Sir Jacob. And I've already added his name to the list of competitors. Now, I am only waiting here for him to arrive. The list is almost full, Morag. Did you add your father's name as well as the name of your uncles?"

"Nay, no' yet. I am no' sure I will since ye said they werena interested in obtainin' the late earl's lands or castle."

"Now, you can't really believe that, can you?" asked Bedivere, surprising her by his words. "After all, don't you think your uncles deserve it? And wouldn't you like your father to own a castle as well?"

"Well, I suppose so," admitted Morag.

"Then come." Bedivere held out his arm. "Allow me to escort you to the practice field where you can add their names to the list before it is too late."

"Do ye really think it is a guid idea?" Morag wasn't sure her uncles would like that, and she was sure her father would hate the idea after he almost didn't let her come back to England.

"I most certainly do. It's a wonderful idea." Bedivere was very convincing.

"But the three of them already said they werena interested," she explained.

"They're being modest," said Bedivere with a deep chuckle.

"But then, what can you expect from the sons of a king? Since they are bastards, they probably don't think they deserve it, but I assure you they do. Matter of fact, I know they will thank you later for adding their names to the list and giving them the chance."

"Aye," added his squire. "I'm sure they'll never forget what you did for them, Morag."

"Never forget," mumbled Morag, pondering the thought.

"Do it," said Branton.

"As my squire, Percival, said, it's a noble act to think of your father and uncles," added Bedivere, making it hard for her to say no.

"Noble," she repeated, thinking of how her sister and cousins had crowns given to them by the late queen. She wanted to feel noble, too.

"You'd better hurry," said Percival.

"I dinna ken," said Morag. "I am no' sure my faither and uncles will like that. Nay." She shook her head. "I'd better no'."

"Come along, Lady Fia." Bedivere's arm remained extended as he took a step closer to her.

"Fia?" Morag scowled at Bedivere, resenting the fact he'd called her by her sister's name again.

"I mean, Maira . . . er, Morag." He continued to hold out his arm. "I am sorry but, for some reason, I keep forgetting your name."

Bedivere watched Morag's brows dip down in frustration and how her mouth pursed in aggravation. He'd purposely called her by her sister and then her cousin's names and made sure to add that he'd forgotten her name when he really

73

hadn't. It was a mean trick, and it didn't sit right with him, but he had to do it. Once the bastard triplets found out they'd been added to the list and entered for consideration, they wouldn't back down. He was sure of it. No man with a lick of pride or a brain in his head would turn away a chance as sweet as this one. The earl's holdings would make someone a very rich man, indeed.

They walked together to the practice yard where Morag wrote her Uncle Rook and Rowen's names on the list, but then stopped and stood up.

"What's the matter?" asked Bedivere.

"There is only one spot left," she said.

"Then use it for your father."

"I dinna see my sister's husband, Conrad's name on the list. I think I'll enter him in the last spot instead."

"Conrad?" asked Sir Bedivere, not expecting her to say this. "Lady Willow's husband?"

"That's right." Morag smiled and bent over, bringing the quill back to the parchment.

Bedivere panicked. He needed all three of the Legendary Bastards there, so Morag had to write down Reed's name in the last spot. Besides, he didn't want Sir Conrad Lochwood there because he would most likely bring his wife. Willow knew Bedivere's secret and would most likely tell Morag when she arrived.

He reached out and clasped his fingers around her hand, not taking the chance that she would ruin his mother's only chance for freedom.

"Sir Conrad will forget about this over time," Bedivere whispered into her ear, pressing up close against her. "But your father . . . he will never forget what you did for him. It will be remembered for the rest of your life."

Feeling like the devil, he brushed his lips up against her hair, and caressed her hand with his. He wasn't sure if it was all part of his scheme or if he did these things because he really liked her. Being so close to her he could smell the hint of heather in her hair and the fresh air of the Scottish hills in her clothes. It made him long to leave England and all his troubles behind him.

The sun broke through the clouds and lit up her strawberry-blond locks with an aura that reminded him of a halo. She was an angel, he decided, and he was the devil. There was no doubt about it. He already regretted deceiving her because he truly did not want to hurt her. However, it was too late because the damage had already been done. Whenever Bedivere set out to convince a woman of something, he never failed.

"All right," she agreed, like he knew she would. "I will sign my father's name to the list in the last spot."

He nodded slightly, watching her write down the last name of the Legendary Bastards of the Crown, sealing his fate as well as the fate of the triplets, though she didn't even know it.

"That's my girl," he mumbled, letting loose of her hand as she scribbled down Reed's name.

"Do ye really think that because of this, I'll never be forgotten?" asked Morag, looking up to him with her big, innocent, brown eyes that seemed to believe every word he said. Of course she'd believe him. After all, she was a gossip and trusted everything she heard without question. She blinked a few times and when their interlocked gazes lasted a little too long, she shyly dropped her focus to the ground.

"Aye, Morag," answered Bedivere, wanting naught more than to stop this premeditated act from happening, but not being able to do so. "I can honestly say that what you just did will never, ever be forgotten."

CHAPTER 7

*S*ir Bedivere stuck so close to Morag the next day that she didn't have a chance to get back to see Mazelina in the secret garden. Neither did she mind, because she loved the attention the man had been giving her all morning. He'd walked her to the chapel and even accompanied her to the ladies solar and waited outside as she talked with the women and stitched. Then he took her for a stroll in the orchard and they stopped to visit the mews where Percival had been spending a lot of time with the birds. It seemed he had a real talent with the hawks and falcons and had offered to help out the falconer in any way he could.

"Allow me," said Bedivere as he pulled out Morag's chair at the dais, helping her to sit.

"Thank ye," said Morag, feeling like a queen as he seated himself next to her between her and Lady Ernestine. "I must admit, I have never had a man pull out a chair for me before now. I'm no' used to it."

"Well, you'll see a lot of that from now on, Lady Morag,"

answered Bedivere with a smile. "I told you I will be your personal guard and escort during your visit here at the castle."

"See Morag? I told you Sir Bedivere was chivalric," Lady Ernestine remarked, taking a sip of wine from her goblet.

"How kind of you to say that," answered Bedivere with a nod of gratitude. He took the platter of meat from the kitchen wench and served Lady Ernestine and then Morag. "Cupbearer, bring more wine for the lady of the castle and Lady Morag please," he said waving down the boy.

"Aye, my lord," said the cupbearer, filling their goblets. When the boy went to fill Bedivere's cup, he stopped him.

"Nay. I'm drinking ale," he told the boy.

"I was pleased to see you arrive to compete for the earl's lands and castle," said Lady Ernestine, leaning over to talk to him. "I have already seen you compete in the sword fight and joust from when you were here vying for Lady Willow's hand in marriage. Therefore, there is no need for you to show me your skills again."

"Aye, and thank you, my lady. If you remember, I won the sword competition," he pointed out as he scooped root vegetables onto their plates and then added a thick brown gravy over their venison.

"You are my guest and a favored one at that," said Ernestine, sounding enamored with him. "You really don't have to serve us, my lord."

"Nonsense. It's my pleasure and the least I can do for the late earl's wife. I want to make sure both his ladies are well taken care of."

"I was only his ward," Morag reminded him, taking a bite of food.

"Sir Bedivere, Morag asked me a question that I wasn't able to answer," Lady Ernestine told him.

"And what would that be?" he asked, taking a swig of ale, his preferred beverage.

"She questioned where your castle was and I couldn't answer because I don't believe I know."

BEDIVERE ALMOST CHOKED on his ale when he heard Lady Ernestine's words. That was one question he wasn't prepared to answer.

"Aye, what is the name of yer castle?" asked Morag, looking up shyly from her goblet. "It must be a big one, since I hear ye are rich."

He was in a bind now and had to say something to suffice them. But if he lied, there were so many knights showing up every day that one of them would smell a rat. As it was, he wasn't sure that word hadn't gotten out about his father's execution and the imprisonment of his family. But this was a chance he had to take. In another week or so, he'd be out of here and headed to safety and a new life with his family in Scotland.

"I currently don't have a castle," he told them, which wasn't a lie. "I tend to travel a lot, and wouldn't have time to tend to matters."

"Oh, so ye have one of those huge manor houses then?" Morag popped a piece of cheese into her mouth.

"Well aye . . . I have . . . a house," he repeated, feeling very hot all of a sudden. He didn't like to be cornered and felt like he was trapped between two women who were going to needle him with questions until he could no longer hold back the truth. "Excuse me, but I believe my squire needs me."

"Yer squire? I dinna even see him," said Morag looking out at the crowd in the great hall. "Where is he?"

"I'll be back," said Bedivere making a beeline for the door. He saw his brother standing in the doorway to the kitchen flirting with a servant. "Percival, come here." He grabbed his brother's arm and hauled him out to the courtyard with him.

"Where are we going?" asked Percival, sounding very grouchy to have been disturbed. "I was just getting to know that buxom kitchen wench."

"You'll have to get to know her at a later date because, right now, we need to come up with a plan of how we're going to save Mother."

"A plan?" Percival licked his lips, savoring the last thing he ate. "You got the girl to sign the bastards up for the competition, so there is nothing we need to do until they arrive."

"Wrong," snapped Bedivere. "And don't talk so loud, someone might hear you. I need you to help me pull off this last job."

"How so? Don't think I'm going to touch a one of the bastards because I won't. I'm not crazy." Percival held out his palms and shook his head. "Personally, I don't see how you're going to take down all three of them by yourself."

"Thank you very much for your vote of confidence, Brother." Bedivere shoved Percival toward the barn.

"Stop pushing," complained the boy. "This is your problem, not mine."

"Don't talk that way! You are part of the family so start acting like it. You are going to help me, like it or not."

"What can I do?"

"I'm not sure, but I'll let you know. In the meantime, I need to find out everything there is to know about the bastard triplets. I need to know their likes, their dislikes, their strengths and their weaknesses. If I'm going to catch them off guard, I need to be a step ahead of them, contemplating their next move."

"How do you plan on doing that?"

"Morag is going to tell me everything I need to know."

"She is?"

"Of course, she won't know it. And I need you to keep that Branton away from her. With the way that girl likes to talk and gossip, I'm sure she'll be my most precious weapon of all."

CHAPTER 8

"*Where* would you like to ride, my lady?" Bedivere sat high on his horse as he escorted Morag to the castle gate the next day right after the main meal.

"I'd like to go down to the creek and see the buds that are startin' to bloom," answered Morag. "I noticed some tiny white flowers the other day and would like to pick a bouquet and bring it back to the castle for Lady Ernestine. She seems so lonely with her husband gone and I'd like to cheer her up."

"Then that's exactly what we'll do." Bedivere led the way with Morag right behind him. As they passed by the tents of the knights who were waiting to apply for the earl's holdings, one of the men looked over to them and called out.

"Bedivere, is that you?" asked the man. "I thought you were locked away? How'd you get out?"

Bedivere quickly looked in the other direction and picked up his pace.

"Sir Bedivere," said Morag, quickly catching up to the man. "That knight was talkin' to ye. Didna ye hear him?"

"I believe you are mistaken. No one was talking to me." He looked straight ahead as he rode.

"Nay, I ken what I heard. He said yer name and somethin' about ye bein' locked up. What did he mean?"

"The men have been well in their cups for the past few days and you need to ignore them, Morag. I don't want you near them unless I am at your side. There is no telling what they might try with a pretty girl like you."

"Do ye really think I'm bonnie?" asked Morag, forgetting all about the knight once Bedivere started talking about her.

"I do," he said, reaching over from atop his horse and stroking the side of her cheek. She closed her eyes partially and leaned in toward him, liking the way it felt. "Now, why don't you show me where those dainty little flowers are that you want to pick?"

"They're right up ahead growin' near the edge of the creek."

"Have you ever raced while riding a horse?"

"Me? Nay. But my cousin, Maira, sits astride the horse and can outride any man."

"I'll bet you can, too."

"I'm sittin' in a sidesaddle like a lady," she pointed out to him. "It's no' befittin' of me to race."

Bedivere looked over his shoulder and then back at her and waggled his eyebrows. "Who is going to know? No one is even looking."

"Do ye think I could?" she asked with a giggle. "I always wanted to race."

"Then do it. I'll even give you a head start since you are at a disadvantage."

"All right, I will." Morag directed her horse into a run, leaving Bedivere in her dust.

She stopped at the edge of the creek and slipped off the horse, falling down onto the bank by the flowers, laughing and trying to regain her breath. Bedivere stopped his horse right behind hers.

"You won," he said, tying the reins of both their horses to the tree and settling down on the ground next to her.

"I didna really win. Ye rode slow on purpose."

"Did I?" he asked with a wry smile.

"Ye are startin' to sound like Mazelina the way ye answer my questions with more questions of yer own."

"Who is Mazelina?" he asked.

Morag slapped her hand over her mouth and sat up. She hadn't meant to tell him that, but it slipped out before she could stop herself. "No one," she said, turning and seeing the flowers. "Oh, are no' they bonnie?" She gathered up a few flowers, snapping them off at the stems and holding them up to her nose. "Take a sniff." She held them out to Bedivere, but noticed he wasn't looking at the flowers. He was staring at her mouth!

Before she knew it, he lifted her chin and pressed his lips gently against hers. Morag felt a warming sensation travel through her body. When Bedivere kissed her, she felt as if she never wanted it to end.

"Do you like that?" he whispered, his hand still on her chin.

"I do," she admitted, noticing the flowers in her hand shaking. He noticed, too.

"Why do you tremble, Morag?" He released her chin. "Do I frighten you?"

"I – I am no' sure," she said, not understanding why this happened to her every time she was near him.

"There is nothing to fear. I promise, I will never hurt you."

"I believe ye," she said, boldly leaning forward and placing her head against his chest. "I dinna ken why Willow said those horrible things about ye because I can see now that they are no' true."

Morag felt Bedivere's body stiffen and didn't understand why he seemed so tense all of a sudden. She sat up and perused him. "Now it seems as if somethin' is frightenin' ye. What is it?"

"Nothing," he said, leaning back and stretching out his legs as he looked up to the clouds in the bright blue sky. "I suppose I just don't like to hear that anyone dislikes me."

"Oh, is that all?" Morag chuckled. "It's only Willow. She is so haughty that I am surprised that Conrad likes her and ended up marryin' her. Dinna worry about it, I'm sure everyone likes ye. How could they no'? Ye are chivalric and honest and protective, and just like the man I want to someday marry."

His eyes snapped over to her and his body stiffened again. "Nay, Morag. You don't want to marry someone like me."

"Why no'?" she asked.

"I'm not right for you. You deserve someone better than me."

"Now who's bein' modest?" she asked, laughing and laying down on the ground, snuggling up to him and looking at the clouds as well. "Have ye ever been married, Bedivere?"

"Nay," he answered after a short pause.

"Why no'? I think any lassie would be proud to have ye as her husband. I would."

Bedivere slipped away from Morag and sat up, feeling very uncomfortable. Morag thought he was the perfect man and even hinted that she wanted to marry him. What had he done? In trying to get close to her to gain information about his next kill, he had made the girl think he was all these things he pretended to be. He hated himself right now, and hated Lord John Whitmore even more for putting him in this position. But if the bastard triplets truly were plotting against King Richard, it was his duty to stop them before they killed the king. He had to find out more.

"I'm sure your father wouldn't like you marrying an Englishman. After all, I hear he hates the English and even hated his own father, King Edward III."

"Aye, so he says," answered Morag, still looking up at the sky. She brought the flowers to her nose as she spoke. "But even though my faither says he hates the English, he is English, so I think it is all an act. He just likes to pretend he's a Scot."

"I would think his hatred for King Edward would have died along with the king. How do your father and your uncles get along with Richard? I'm sure Richard, being of true noble blood, hasn't quite accepted bastard uncles."

"True," she said.

Good. Now Bedivere was getting somewhere. If it sounded at all like the triplets hated or despised Richard, he'd have his answer. Mayhap, they truly were plotting to kill the king.

"True? So you mean . . . they hate Richard?"

"Oh, nay, no' at all. As a matter of fact, Richard had a hard time acceptin' them and doesna really talk to my faither or uncles at all. But they like him just fine. They understand how hard it must be for Richard since his grandfaither ended up havin' a better relationship with my Uncles Rook and Reed than he did with his own grandson."

"What about your father?"

"What about him?"

"Does your father hold resentment for Richard?"

"No' at all. He likes Scotland and doesna want to bother himself with anythin' to do with the English. Sometimes he sounds gruff, but my faither doesna mean it."

"So he would never fight against the English king?"

"He will fight with Scotland if the English attack, aye, of course. But remember, King Richard is my cousin. My sister and Willow and Maira and I have spent time with him and that is guid enough for my faither and uncles. They like that we sometimes spend time at court even though they have no desire to go there since Edward died."

"Really," he said, cocking his head. "But isn't it every man's wish to have more? If your father and uncles were spawns of the late King Edward, mayhap they would . . . I don't know . . . possibly want to sit on the English throne themselves?"

Morag laughed at that. "Oh, nay. That is the last thing they'd ever want."

"Why would you say that?"

"Because I oftentimes hear them talkin' and sayin' they feel sorry for Richard."

"Sorry for him? Why?"

"My Uncle Rowen was once a pirate and loves to live by the sea. Uncle Rook used to live underground in the catacombs and is happy now just being a knight."

"What about your father?"

"My faither doesna care about sittin' on a throne. He loves

the Highlands and wants to stay as far away from England as possible."

"So, they really have no desire for more riches." Bedivere pondered the thought.

"Before, when they were kent as the Demon Thief and raided the king, it was because of vengeance against Edward wantin' them killed as babies. But that is over now and they have changed. I dinna even ken why I wrote their names on the list because if they said they didna want the earl's castle and lands then they meant it. I'm afeard I have just taken three spots from some lords who really want what the earl left behind."

"Thank you for telling me that, Morag," said Bedivere, realizing by Morag's words that the bastard triplets were most likely not plotting to kill Richard after all. And after hearing this, he wondered if, perhaps, Lord Whitmore received bad information.

"Look at that cloud," said Morag. "It reminds me of Ben Nevis."

"Who?" asked Bedivere, not even paying attention.

"The highest mountain in Scotland." She sat up and looked at him with excitement in her eyes. "Havena ye ever climbed it? I will have to take ye there someday."

"Aye, you do that," he said.

"What do ye see in the clouds, Bedivere?"

"I see rainclouds and suggest we get back to the castle quickly or you're going to get wet."

"Nay, I dinna think it is goin' to rain."

Just as she said that, a clap of thunder rattled the sky and big drops of cold rain fell against her face.

"Ye're right, as always. Let's go," she said, running for her horse.

He helped her into the saddle and was about to mount his own horse when she called out.

"Wait! I forgot the flowers."

"I'll get them," he said, hurrying back to pick up the flowers, taking a moment to sniff them before heading back to the horses. He knew now he couldn't kill Morag's father and uncles. By Morag's words and the feeling in his gut, he felt as if he'd been fed a lie. He needed to stop this nonsense before innocent people got killed. But he wasn't sure how he was going to tell Lord Whitmore that the Legendary Bastards of the Crown were not going to die by his hand after all.

CHAPTER 9

As much as Morag enjoyed the time she'd been spending with Sir Bedivere, it had been three days now since she'd been to the secret garden.

Everywhere she went, Sir Bedivere had accompanied her. She never realized how much the man liked to talk. He asked her about her father and her family and even about her uncles. He was very interested in her, more so than anyone had ever been before. She liked that. Most men only talked about themselves. Bedivere made her feel more important than anything in his own life. The more time she spent with him, the more she felt like he was the man she wanted to marry, even though he told her she deserved someone better than him.

Getting up before the sun rose, she hurried to the stable, and once again snuck out the postern gate and headed for the secret garden. Each day, the grounds in front of the castle were getting more and more crowded with tents, horses, knights, and squires that were waiting for the start of the festivities. Villagers filled the area trying to sell their wares.

Tumblers and jugglers entertained the visitors. There was even a bonfire lit outside the castle every night with men drinking and dancing to the music of the strolling musicians. Every man on the list wanted to get his time with Lady Ernestine, trying to convince her that he deserved to be awarded the earl's castle and lands.

She highly expected her uncles to arrive any day now. Lady Ernestine had sent special messengers to Whitehaven and Naward to tell Rowen and Rook that they were now on the list and being considered as possible recipients of the late earl's holdings. She figured she could talk her way out of being reprimanded by them since they both truly would be perfect choices for the prize.

However, what really concerned her was how her father was going to react. After the last missive sent to Scotland, she wasn't sure he wouldn't kill the messenger this time. Thankfully, she had talked Branton into going along with the messenger to help keep her father's anger at bay. Hopefully, Branton could convince him to come to Rothbury after all. Morag told him to do whatever it took to convince her father to join her here.

She headed away from the castle, feeling the cool morning air against her skin. Never had she felt so alive. Her time with Bedivere was exciting and intriguing. Instead of feeling lonely and worthless, she felt completed and beautiful when she was with him. Morag really liked the man and hoped that he would try to kiss her again soon because all she could think about was being in his strong, protective arms.

Anxious to tell Mazelina about Bedivere, Morag rode like the wind, not even aware that she was being watched from the battlements.

* * *

"Where does she go?" Bedivere asked Percival, leaning on the battlements, straining his eyes to see Morag in the dark.

"Who are you talking about?" Percival yawned and leaned back against the wall with his eyes closed. "And why did you drag me up here so early in the morning? I wasn't done sleeping yet."

"I'm talking about Morag," said Bedivere, watching as the girl rode unescorted straight into the dark woods. "What the hell is she thinking? It's not safe out there. She doesn't even have that squirrely squire with her for protection. I don't like it at all."

"Branton's been sent to Scotland to collect Morag's father and bring him back here." Percival pushed his long, blond hair back and tied it in a queue. "Face it, Brother, Morag might not be safe in the woods all alone, but she's not safe with you either."

"Not true." Bedivere stood up straight, his hands balling to fists as he tried to ignore the anger pulsing through his veins. "I would never hurt her. You need to know that. Morag is a special girl. She is an angel to me."

"An angel?" Percival chuckled. "It sounds to me like all the time you've been spending with her has addled your brain. You are smitten with the wench, aren't you?"

"Mayhap. What does it matter?"

"It matters because you have played her like a lute to pump information out of her so you can kill her father and uncles."

"Quiet," snapped Bedivere. "How many times do I have to tell you to keep your mouth shut about the mission?" His eyes flicked back and forth making sure the guards at the end of the wall walk hadn't heard them.

"You've got yourself into a very awkward predicament," said Percival, his eyes closing as he spoke. "You say you care for her and want to protect her and that you would never hurt her."

"Aye. That's true."

"Then don't let her find out who you really are or what you're about to do or she's going to be more than hurt. She'll want to kill you!"

Bedivere realized what Percival said was true. He had let his walls of protection down whenever he was around Morag and that was something he hadn't done in a very long time now. Ever since he'd turned into an assassin, he'd learned to hide his feelings, burying them deep within himself to the point that he had started to think they didn't exist anymore. After killing eleven men, he felt numb, and thought caring about anyone besides his family would never happen again. But now, he was no longer sure because he truly cared what happened to Morag.

"Percival, these past few days, I've been able to collect information from Morag about her father and uncles."

"Good. So now you know how you'll . . . do it?" Percival fell asleep against the wall and let out a loud snore.

"Wake up, you fool." Bedivere slapped his brother on the shoulder, causing Percival to almost fall over, but catching himself before he hit the ground.

"What? What is it?" Percival's eyes opened wide in confusion and he grabbed for his dagger, acting like he thought they were being attacked.

"Wake up! And God's eyes, put away the blade. We're not

being attacked, but I've got an important job for you to do. That is why I called you up here."

"Job? What job?" Percival looked at the dagger and shrugged, then shoved it back into his waist belt.

"Since you're my contact this time, I need you to go straight back to Whitmore and tell him I've changed my mind."

"Changed your mind? About what?"

"The . . . job," Bedivere said under his breath, his eyes glancing over to the guards once again.

"You can't be serious!" said Percival. "You want me to give him that message? If I do that, I'll be the next one on your list, I guarantee it."

"Tell him I think he got some bad information and that I won't go through with it."

"And what about Mother? You'd risk her life because of a girl? After all, we both know it's the reason you are hesitating to fulfill your commitment."

Bedivere paced back and forth. Percival made sense. He couldn't take the chance that his mother would be killed because of him refusing to do a job. He looked out over the battlements and then back to his brother.

"Before you go to Whitmore, stop by at the cottage. Tell Aunt Joan and Uncle Theobald to take our siblings and go into hiding."

"What are you saying? How do you expect them to disappear and not have Whitmore notice?"

"You said they have friends in the village. Mayhap, they can help them."

"Mayhap, but what happens when Whitmore finds out?"

"It shouldn't matter. I already earned their freedom. He can't stop them from leaving."

"And what about Mother?"

Bedivere rubbed his hand over his face. He didn't want to make this choice. He wouldn't let his mother die, but neither would he kill Morag's father and uncles when he didn't believe they were guilty of plotting against the king.

"Tell him it was one kill for every person I saved. This is three, and that's not fair."

"So am I telling him you'll do one but not three? Or am I telling him that you'll not do any at all?"

"We'll make him believe I'll do one more like we'd agreed upon. But let him choose which one of the three is my next mark."

"So you're really going to go through with it?"

"Nay, you fool, I'm not! But Whitmore doesn't need to know that. If he thinks I'll do away with one of the three, it'll buy us some time until I figure out how to save Mother. Once I figure out that part, we'll join the rest of our family and head to Scotland."

"Bedivere, what is happening to you? I've never known you to run from your troubles."

"I'm not running from anything. I'm just going to remove my family from this unfortunate situation once and for all."

"All right then. I'll go and give the message, but I think that wench has done something to make you want to run."

In a way, Bedivere thought the same thing, but he wouldn't admit it. He felt himself falling hard for Morag but he knew it could never work between them. Once she found out from her sister about his past, Morag would hate him, fear him, and want nothing to do with him ever again. That thought alone was enough to make him want to run. But no matter how fast or far he ran, he would never be able to escape his horrible past.

* * *

ENTERING the secret garden just as the sky started to lighten on the horizon, Morag hurried to the cottage, hoping to find Mazelina there.

"Mazelina, I'm here," she said, barging into the house without knocking, not thinking until afterwards that the old woman might want her privacy. "Mazelina?" She looked over at the bed, but the woman wasn't there.

Curious, she moved through the house looking for evidence of the woman's personal items, clothes, or perhaps even food on the table or in the cupboards, but found nothing. Mazelina wasn't here. Morag had waited too long to return and now she'd been abandoned.

Sadly, she turned to go but stopped dead in her tracks when she saw the old woman standing by the door.

"Mazelina, I didna see ye outside nor did I hear ye come into the house."

"So you returned?" asked the old woman, holding her hands folded in front of her as she stood still.

"Aye, I am here for my trainin'. I am sorry I missed a few days but I've been busy."

"I know. With Sir Bedivere."

Morag hadn't planned on telling the woman that but it didn't matter. Once again, she read Morag's mind.

"Aye, with Sir Bedivere," she answered with a sigh. "I'm

afraid I am fallin' in love with the man. Do ye think that's wrong?"

"Love? Didn't you tell me that you didn't think love was important?" Once again, Mazelina answered Morag's questions with her own questions. Morag wished she would stop that and be more like Imanie.

"I said love wasna important in a marriage. But this is different."

"How so?"

"It's different because . . . because we are no' betrothed to be married."

"You wish to marry him, don't you?"

Morag's eyes snapped up and she sank down atop a chair as the old woman strolled toward her. "I do. I dinna understand it. It all happened so fast. But Sir Bedivere is the perfect man." Morag smiled and gazed up into the air as she continued. "He is handsome and kind and verra thoughtful. He is chivalric and treats me like a queen. He cares about me and also the people in my life. He is strong and protective of me in every way."

"And you like that?"

Morag nodded slightly. "Of course, I do. What lassie wouldna?"

"Your head says all these things about a man you barely know. But what does your heart tell you?"

"I dinna ken what ye mean." Morag wrapped her arms around in herself in a protective hug. "My heart can see that he's a guid man. I'm sure my faither will see that, too, in time."

"Do you really think so? What do you know about Bedivere? And will your father honestly accept the fact that you have fallen in love with a Sassenach?"

When Mazelina said the word Sassenach, a shudder ran through Morag. She pictured her father's face and his warning before she left. It was doubtful he would support a union between Bedivere and her. Mayhap thinking she could marry Sir Bedivere was only a silly dream on her part. Suddenly, Morag wasn't feeling as confident as she had when she first came here today. "Mazelina, ye sound as if ye ken somethin' about Bedivere that I dinna ken. What is it?"

"If I told you all I know, wouldn't that be gossiping? The exact thing you are trying not to do?"

"Nay," she said, slapping her hands atop the table. "It's no' gossip if the story is true. Tell me."

"My ability to read into people's minds is a curse as well as a blessing. Just like anything in life, too much of a good thing can turn bad quickly if you misuse it."

"Mazelina, ye dinna make any sense and are confusin' me again. Are ye sayin' Sir Bedivere is a guid man or a bad one?"

"That, my dear, is for you to find out. I'll ask you again, what do you really know about the man?"

"Well, I ken that . . . I mean he is . . . he comes from . . ." Suddenly, Morag realized that she knew nothing about Bedivere at all. They had spent all their time talking about her and her father and uncles that she never thought to ask about him. The only things she knew of him were the ones that she heard as gossip. "I suppose we spent so much time talkin' about me that I didna have time to ask much about him."

"Morag! Lady Morag, are you in here?"

"It's Bedivere!" exclaimed Morag, jumping up and running to look out the door. Sure enough, in the light of the rising sun, she saw Bedivere leading his horse into the secret garden.

"Nay," mumbled Morag. "He wasna supposed to follow me here. I canna let him see ye, Mazelina."

"Don't worry about that," said the old woman, stepping back into a shadow. "Go to him, Morag."

"But we didna even have my lesson yet. I dinna want to leave before I've learned somethin' from ye."

"You have."

"I have?" Morag looked back over her shoulder at the woman in confusion. "Nay, I havena. What did ye teach me?"

"Think about it," said Mazelina. "There are some things you have to learn on your own."

"Morag, where are you?" called out Bedivere, coming closer to the house.

"I'll distract him and willna let him come into the cottage so he doesna see ye," Morag told Mazelina. The woman didn't answer. "Mazelina?" Morag looked back, but didn't see the woman anywhere. Figuring she was hiding from Bedivere for some reason that Morag didn't understand, she stepped out onto the porch and waved her hand in the air. "I'm here, Bedivere," she said, hurrying down the stairs to meet him.

"What is this place?" asked Bedivere, glancing at the surroundings. "And why are you here?"

"It's a place I come to think and to be . . . alone," she told him, hoping he couldn't read minds like Mazelina or he would know her secret.

"Well, I don't like it. It's not safe for you to be unescorted and out in the woods in the dark."

"Ye sound as if ye care." She walked back to the gate with him as she spoke.

"I do care, Morag. I care for you very much."

"Do ye really?"

"Of course. And I want you to know that I would never purposely ever hurt you." He took her hands in his and stared into her eyes. Then he leaned forward and kissed her on the mouth.

Morag tried to listen to her heart, the way Mazelina told her to do. She didn't feel anything bad about him. Mayhap Bedivere was a little mysterious, but she believed him when he said he cared for her and also when he said he would protect her and never hurt her. Still, mayhap, she needed to test him. Perhaps then she would see if he meant what he said or if he was playing her for a fool.

"If ye mean what ye say . . . then marry me."

"What?" He dropped her hands and stepped back. "Why would you say that, Morag? You don't mean it."

"I told ye I wanted to marry someone like ye, and I do mean it. I want ye. Now, what do ye say?"

"This is all so sudden," he replied, nervously dragging a hand through his hair. "And your father is sure not to agree to the marriage."

"I dinna need him to agree. It doesna matter."

"Oh, I see. You have been granted the right to marry the man of your choice, just like your sister and cousins."

She could have corrected him right there, but something made her keep her mouth shut. Longing in her heart for Bedivere made her want him more than she'd ever wanted any man before. True, her father wouldn't like the idea, but he'd get used to it over time. Besides, what did it matter? Marrying an Englishman would be a great alliance. Anyone could see that.

"Will ye marry me?" she asked again.

"I don't know. Mayhap," he said.

"I dinna like that answer. It makes me think everythin' between us has been a lie. Have ye been lyin' to me, Bedivere?"

Bedivere swallowed forcefully, feeling tongue-tied and choked. He never expected Morag to be so bold as to come out and ask him to marry her. She was quite the girl. Most men would be put off by an action so brash by a woman. Then again, most women wanted naught to do with him and it was touching that she liked him enough to want to be his wife.

Would she feel the same way if she knew he was an assassin? Or would he even have to tell her? Something like this would surely be a wedge between them. If her father ever found out, he would probably kill him. His heart ached because he wished things were different. If he wasn't an assassin and, instead, a respectable knight, he'd jump at the chance to marry Morag. But sadly, he realized she deserved someone so much better than him.

"Bedivere?" Her soft, lithe voice floated on the breeze like a chirp of a fragile meadow pipit. "I think I am fallin' in love with ye."

"Y-you are?" This was something else he never expected to hear. Had he played his hand too hard? In purposely trying to get close to Morag to find out information about the bastard triplets, mayhap he'd overdone it a bit. Then again, he felt the same way about her, so perhaps the feelings between them were real. "I don't know what to say." He pulled her close to him and held her protectively against his chest. Ironic, that the man who was ordered to kill her father was also the one she trusted with her life.

"Say we'll be married, Bedivere. At least, let's get betrothed. I am sure I can change my faither's mind. As soon as he meets ye, he'll see what an honorable man ye are."

"I'm not so sure about that," he said, kissing the top of her head and staring out into the secret garden.

"If ye're worried because of yer reputation with my cousin, Willow, dinna be. I will talk to her about ye and she will clear yer name."

"Nay!" he said, releasing her quickly and stepping away. "Don't talk to Willow. There's no need."

"There isna? Why no'?" she asked, looking at him suspiciously. "Bedivere, is there somethin' ye are keepin' from me? Did somethin' happen between ye and Willow? I ken what a flirt she is and it is her reputation around the men that she should be worried about."

"Nay, nothing happened between us, I swear. I mean, beside a small, meaningless kiss. I just meant there is no need to talk to her because . . . because I think we should get betrothed."

"Ye do?" Morag's eyes opened wide and her face lit up in joy. "I accept, Bedivere. I canna wait to be yer wife." She threw her arms around him and squeezed him tightly.

Bedivere froze. What the hell just happened? Why did he tell her he would marry her when he knew he could not? He was an assassin, and she was the granddaughter of the late king, not to mention the daughter of a man who was a legend in his own time. He'd had a weak moment, liking the thought of someone loving him. But now, he realized he was going to have to break Morag's heart. He didn't deserve her, and he hadn't been honest with her. Nay, he couldn't marry her, but neither could he tell her that now. She was much too excited.

"Perhaps, we should keep our betrothal to ourselves for now."

"Oh, ye're worried about my faither, I see."

"Aye," he said, for lack of knowing what else to say.

"All right, we'll keep it a secret until I can talk to my da and explain to him what a wonderful man ye are."

"You do that," he said, escorting her to her horse, wondering how he was going to get out of this mess. After helping her mount, he got atop his horse and, from the corner of his eye, he thought he saw someone in the garden. His head jerked upward. "Who's that?" he asked, his hand reaching for his sword.

"Did ye see someone, Bedivere?" Morag looked over to the cottage and then back to him. "I dinna see anyone."

Bedivere scanned the area, realizing he must have imagined it. If anyone had been out there, he'd see them since it was in the middle of a dead garden with nowhere for them to hide.

"Nay, my mistake," he said, turning and heading out of the garden, still thinking about the betrothal. Now, he wished that he had never followed Morag here at all.

CHAPTER 10

"*B*edivere, I dinna understand why we canna at least tell Lady Ernestine about our betrothal." Morag walked hand in hand with Bedivere the next day as they strolled through the orchard. Since there were so many knights that had already arrived for the competition, Lady Ernestine had started to take audiences with them. She also spent time in the practice yard watching them spar and joust.

"Nay, she's too busy and we wouldn't want to distract her." Bedivere scanned the courtyard. Everyone seemed to be looking at him. Mayhap it was his imagination, but still it was too risky. Someone might approach him like the man who called out to him, knowing he and his family had been imprisoned. Nothing was a secret for long, and that only made him anxious to finish off his mission in exchange for the release of his mother. But now, that wasn't even an option because he refused to eliminate Morag's father or uncles.

"Here she comes now," said Morag, waving to Lady Ernestine. The woman made her way over to them, stopping twice to greet some of the competitors along the way.

"Morag, I have a favor to ask of you," said Lady Ernestine.

"Of course," she said cheerfully, too cheerful for Bedivere's liking. In his opinion, when anyone asked for a favor it was always bad news.

"I have personally invited fifty of my late husband's most eligible barons and knights to compete for his holdings. However, I am finding it hard to choose. I was hoping that you could sit in with me for the next few days while I listen to what the competitors have to say."

"Ye want me to do that?" asked Morag, her eyes sparkling with excitement. "I can help ye make the decision which men should be presented to the king to inherit the earl's holdin's?"

"Aye. I trust your judgment, even though I know that you are going to tend to favor your father and uncles, and possibly Sir Bedivere, too." She smiled slyly.

"Well, I might tend to favor Sir Bedivere since we are now betrothed."

"Morag!" Bedivere felt like hiding under a rock. Why did Morag have to tell her this when they'd just discussed that they would keep it to themselves?

"You are betrothed?" asked the lady of the castle in surprise. "My, that was fast! Congratulations to the both of you."

"Bedivere, I ken I was supposed to keep it a secret, but I had to tell Lady Ernestine," Morag apologized. "I am so excited to be gettin' married and had to share it with her since she has been like a mathair to me while I lived here." Morag held on to his arms and looked up to him with those big, brown, innocent eyes. He found it hard to be angry. The girl was excited and meant no harm. He should have known that Morag could not keep a secret.

"Secret?" asked Lady Ernestine. "Why on earth would you want to do that? I will have the wedding banns posted right away to announce it." She took Morag's hands in hers. "We don't have to wait the required three weeks. As a matter of fact, I think you should marry Sir Bedivere right here at Rothbury before I give away my husband's holdings. After all, this has been your home for years now, too. Not to mention, we already have the crowd to help you celebrate," she added with a chuckle.

"Aye, I'd like that," said Morag, looking over to Bedivere. "Can we do that, Bedivere? Please?"

"Morag," he said in a low voice, noticing the crowd gathering around them and eavesdropping. "Remember, the whole reason we weren't telling anyone was because of your father."

"Och, that's right," said Morag, hitting her head with a thump. "I was so excited that I forgot, I need to talk to Da first."

"Then, mayhap, we'd better keep it hushed until you discuss it with your father," said Lady Ernestine with an understanding nod. "After all, we all know how adamant he is that his daughters marry Scotsmen. Good thing Fia married a Scot."

"Aye, good for her," mumbled Bedivere, dreading the meeting with Reed Douglas that would be unavoidable.

"Come, my dear, everyone is waiting for us." Lady Ernestine's voice held excitement as well as a hint of sadness.

Morag looked back at Bedivere and he could see the confusion in her eyes.

"Go," he told her.

"But what about our walk? We were goin' to sit on the grass in the orchard to eat."

"We can do that later."

"But what about ye?" asked Morag. "What will ye do?"

"Oh, I'll find something to do, don't worry." He leaned over and kissed Morag on the head and turned to go to his solar to think. If he was going to marry Morag, save his mother, and avoid having to kill the bastard triplets, he was going to need nothing short of a miracle. Unfortunately, he didn't believe God smiled on men like him, so a miracle was out of the question right now. He'd have to find another option.

MORAG SPENT two days with Lady Ernestine, listening to men brag as they talked about themselves. Each tried to convince the lady of the castle that he should be the one to inherit the late earl's fiefdom. After spending the mornings listening to braggarts, Morag went to the practice yard and sat with Lady Ernestine each afternoon as they watched pompous men sparring to show off their skill with weapons.

Morag yawned, being bored by the entire process.

"What do you think, my dear?" asked Lady Ernestine, leaning over in the lists to speak to her.

"About what?" Morag's thoughts had drifted and she found it hard to focus on what she was doing. First, she could think of naught else but Bedivere, and then she started thinking about her visit with Mazelina.

"I think Lord Henry from Devon is a good candidate, as well as Baron Oxford from Suffolk. Don't you?"

"What about Sir Bedivere?" asked Morag. "Or mayhap my uncles or even my faither?"

"Of course, they are also good choices, too. But until I

speak with them, I can't consider them. After all, your father and uncles have yet to arrive. For all I know, they are not interested at all."

"They'll be here soon," Morag assured her, not really knowing if they'd show up. Right now, Morag wished for Fia or her cousins to be there so she could tell them about her betrothal to Bedivere. She supposed she could go back and talk to Mazelina, but the old woman confused Morag. After their last two meetings, Morag had left the secret garden feeling like she was in a daze.

"Is something bothering you, my dear?" Lady Ernestine applauded for the two men who had just finished jousting. Morag clapped as well, but her heart wasn't in it.

"Aye," admitted Morag. "Somethin' is botherin' me. Lady Ernestine, do ye think Sir Bedivere would make a good husband for me?"

The woman laughed. "I thought you already had decided he would. If not, why did you two get betrothed? Was it for alliances?"

"I suppose I acted hastily, and I canna say it was for alliances since I dinna even ken where he lives or anythin' about his personal life."

"Then you need to find out these things before it is too late," suggested the woman.

"How?" asked Morag. "I feel as if I need my sister and cousins to tell me what to do. I wrote and sent a missive to my cousin, Willow, asking for advice."

"Now, Morag," said Lady Ernestine, laying her hand atop Morag's. "You don't need your sister or cousins to tell you how you feel about a man. But if you want to get to know him better, you will need time alone with him. After all, I have kept you very busy lately and, for that, I am sorry."

"No need to apologize. I am happy to be here although I'm no' sure I have been much help."

"Go to him," said the woman with caring in her eyes. "Spend time with him and then you will know if he is the one for you or not."

"Thank ye, Lady Ernestine." Morag got up to leave. "I value yer guidance, as I dinna seem able to look into a person's heart the way ye were able to do with the earl."

"My husband was a gruff man at times, but we had a good marriage."

"What makes a guid marriage?" asked Morag curiously.

The woman thought for a minute and then held up a finger. "I would have to say honesty is one of the biggest things that will make or break a marriage. If there is not open communication between a husband and wife, then there will never be trust between you. And without trust, there will never be true love."

CHAPTER 11

*B*edivere wiped the water from his face, having shaved off his mustache and beard. Then he ran his fingers over the array of weapons, feeling as if he no longer knew who he was. Picking up one of his sharpest daggers, he looked at his reflection in the blade, somehow hoping things would be different this time. Once again, the flames of the hearth lit up his face in an orange glow. He still looked like the devil, even without his beard and mustache and the fact he tried to feel like a new man.

He had taken the last two days to think, staying away from Morag and all the activity in the courtyard, waiting for his brother to return with word from Whitmore. It was a good thing Lady Ernestine kept Morag busy, because he didn't know how to tell the girl that he couldn't marry her after all. That was not a task he was looking forward to doing. Still, it needed to be done. Morag would never be happy with a man like him. And he couldn't marry her without telling her he was an assassin. Nay, he decided, that was something he could never do. He didn't want her high opinion of him to ever be tainted by the true facts of his miserable life.

Bedivere felt like a recluse locked away in his chamber, not even going to the great hall for his meals. Instead, he'd instructed a kitchen boy to bring his food to his room on a tray where he'd eat in private. All alone. A steaming tub of water awaited him near the fire, ready to wash away his sins. As soon as the boy delivered his food, he planned on eating while he soaked his body, trying to cleanse the blackness of his dark soul.

His heart felt empty like never before. Two years ago, things had been different. His father was a knight, wanting to climb the ranks. That's when he befriended Sir John Whitmore, who had just been made advisor to the king. The next thing Bedivere knew, his father was accused of plotting to kill King Richard.

Bedivere and his family watched in horror one day while Whitmore hung Sir Gilbert Hamilton in the privacy of his own castle's courtyard. Of course, Bedivere tried to stop his father's execution, knowing the man could never do something as horrible as what he'd been accused of doing. However, he couldn't prove it either, and had no time to try.

Bedivere's action of fighting against Whitmore only made things worse. That day, his entire family was punished because he had fought to save his father's life. In anger, Whitmore threw even his mother, aunt, and his young siblings into the dungeon. Only by agreeing to be the king's assassin was Bedivere able to free his family one by one. Most of his family, that is. His mother still remained imprisoned, waiting for Bedivere to do his last job in order to set her free.

In anger of the man he'd become, Bedivere squeezed the

blade of destruction in his palm until he bled. "Damn it," he spat, standing and throwing the dagger atop the pile with the other weapons he'd used to take the lives of nearly a dozen men. He couldn't help wondering, did those men deserve to die? He'd been told they were plotting the king's assassination and that they had to be stopped and couldn't be trusted. But was it true?

At the time, Bedivere didn't know and neither did it matter. All he cared about was protecting his family. He was the man of the household since the death of his father, and it was his responsibility to continue on in his father's wake.

A knock at the door startled him, dragging him from his self-inflicting thoughts.

"Just a moment," he called out, knowing it was the kitchen boy with his food. Quickly throwing a blanket over the weapons, he found a strip of cloth in his travel bag and wound it around his bleeding hand. Then he headed over to the door and pulled it open.

Morag stood there, balancing a tray of food on one hand and clutching the neck of a bottle of wine with the other.

"Hello, Bedivere. Did ye miss me?" Her smile lit up the room and her beauty left him short of breath. Something about Morag made him forget his troubles even if it was only momentarily. Her presence in his life gave him hope that someday he could change and that he could escape his troubled past.

"Morag," he mumbled, his heart beating rapidly at the mere sight of his angel. He never felt this nervous, not even the first time he'd been sent out on his first kill. Something about being around Morag made him anxious, excited, and a little bit scared.

"Well, are ye goin' to invite me in or are we goin' to stand here all night until I drop the food at yer feet? The tray is heavy." She looked down to the tray and it wobbled, threatening to spill.

Bedivere's hand shot out, taking it from her. Still, he blocked her path into the room. "Thank you for delivering my food, but you really didn't have to do this." He reached for the bottle of wine next, but she pushed his hand away and snuck under his arm, entering the room.

"Nonsense. I saw the kitchen boy comin' to yer chamber so I told him I would deliver the food to ye."

"Why?" he asked, turning around as she spotted the tub and made her way further into the room. Knowing it was going to be impossible to get rid of her, he sighed and closed the door.

"Why no'?" she asked him.

"Morag, you shouldn't be in my chamber unescorted and with the door closed." He felt a little contradictive since he had been the one to close the door. He could have very well left it open to avoid the rumors on the morrow.

"Really." Her eyes shot over to the closed door and she smiled. "I havena eaten yet, so I thought we could share the food." She put the wine bottle down on the table and motioned with her hand. "Hurry, bring it over before it gets cold. I convinced the cook to give me an extra servin' of venison and gravy, plus one of the loaves of freshly-baked white bread."

"You did, did you?" Bedivere chuckled and brought the tray over and placed it on the table. "I thought you said you intercepted the kitchen boy on his way up here."

"Did I say that?" She held a hand to her mouth. "I might

have stretched the truth a little, but it was only because I wanted to be alone with ye. Since ye havena been out of yer room in days, this was the only way I was ever goin' to see ye."

"I'm sorry, but I just needed time alone. To think."

"Well, mayhap, we can think together."

"Once the word gets out that we were behind closed doors together, what is going to happen then?"

"Only the cook and the kitchen boy ken about it."

"Only? Morag, they are two people who talk to a hundred others every day."

"Then let their tongues wag, I dinna care." Morag uncovered the platter and closed her eyes as she took a whiff of the food. "It doesna matter to me what others say about me behind my back. Does it bother ye what they say about ye?"

"Nay, I suppose not," he answered, knowing they could be saying a lot worse. If they were busy gossiping about how he had a lady in his room, they wouldn't be talking about his other shady activities. "Well, let's eat."

He sat down and grabbed for the bread, but her hand shot out and her fingers gripped tightly around his wrist.

"Ye're bleedin'."

"I . . . cut myself while shaving," he lied, already feeling bad but not able to tell her the truth. She wouldn't understand that he rid himself of the facial hair because he saw himself as the devil. Nay, that would only cause her to ask too many other questions that he didn't want to answer.

"I like it," she said, taking a bite of venison, studying his face. She reached out and ran her fingertips against his smooth jawline. "Yer skin feels so soft."

God's eyes, didn't she know what she was doing to him?

Every time she touched him it made him want to take her to his bed.

"I'll take some wine now," he said, picking up the bottle and looking around. "We don't seem to have a goblet."

"We dinna need one," she answered, grabbing the bottle from him and taking a swig. "Just do it like that. We can share." She handed the bottle back to him.

"Aye," he said, raising the bottle to drink, tasting the sweet essence of her lips on the rim and wanting to taste them directly instead.

"I see ye had a bath prepared. And I still see steam comin' off the water."

"I haven't had a chance to use it yet. I was going to sit in the tub and eat my meal, but I won't be doing that now."

"Why no'?" she asked. "Dinna let me stop ye." The naughty playfulness of her words reflected in the sparkle of her eyes. What kind of dangerous game was she playing with him, daring him to undress while she was in the room?

"Quit acting like a temptress, my little fey."

"Fey?" She looked up with her big doe eyes and blinked.

"Don't act so innocent. If you want to join me in the tub, then just say so."

"Join ye?" Her eyes darted over to the tub and then back to him. "Nay, of course no', dinna be silly. I just meant that I didna want to stop ye from whatever ye were doin' when I arrived."

Actually, he welcomed her intrusion because now he had something else to think about instead of his dilemma.

"I suggest we eat our food. Mayhap when I'm done, I'll have my wine in the tub as I relax by the fire."

"Of course, my lord." She smiled slightly and looked down

to the food, no longer able to meet his gaze. She had never called him my lord before, so he knew she was nervous. Had she come here purposely to share his bed? And if she stayed, would either of them regret it in the morning? He wasn't sure about anything anymore.

"You never told me what you were doing in that garden." The food was delicious. His favorite meal was venison with a rich, brown gravy. Also on the tray besides the bread were pickled beets and what looked like an apple tart.

"I was there to think," she told him. "Just the same as ye've been doin' for the past few days locked away in yer chamber."

"I beg to differ. I am sure it isn't the same at all."

Her hand stilled and she kept her focus on the table. That told him she was lying. He could have questioned her about it again, but decided, what did it matter? After all, he'd been lying to her, too. Mayhap, if they were both liars they did belong together after all.

He encouraged small talk as they ate, asking about the other knights and how their audiences with Lady Ernestine went. They shared a few laughs and talked about nothing of importance. Then, right when he was getting ready to tell her he had to break the betrothal, she got up and stretched and headed over to the fire.

"Why dinna we sit down by the fire on this blanket?" she asked, making Bedivere jump up and run over to the hearth. His weapons were under there and he didn't want her to see them. She reached for the blanket, and he realized he had to cause a distraction quickly or she was going to find out who he was.

So, doing the only thing he could think of that would get

her mind off of the blanket, he pulled her into his arms and kissed her.

"Mmmm," she said, with her head tilting back and her eyes half-closed. "I like that."

"So do I," he admitted, having lustful thoughts again.

"Take off yer clothes," she told him.

"What?" He jerked away from her as if he were burned.

"I willna look. Go ahead and get in the water before it gets cold. I'll bring yer wine to ye."

"Oh," he said, sadly realizing she had no intention of doing anything other than keeping him company. He supposed it was better this way. "If you insist," he said, eager to get in the water so she wouldn't see his hardened manhood poking at his breeches. In one fluid motion, he undressed and entered the tub, slipping down below the surface.

Morag couldn't help herself. She peeked over her shoulder to see the bare backside of Bedivere as he stepped into the tub. His body had no fat, but pure muscles. He was long and lean and his naked back end looked enticing. And when he raised his leg to step into the tub, she saw his engorged manhood, straight as an arrow. She gasped, glad he had dunked under the water or he would have heard her and known she had spied. It was clear to her now that Bedivere wanted her as much as she wanted him.

Grabbing the bottle of wine, she headed over to the tub just as Bedivere emerged, spouting water at her, hitting her in the eye.

"Ye cur!" Squinting one eye, Morag hit him with her free hand. But his hands shot out to grab her. She squirmed to get away, but her hair hung over her eyes, blocking her view.

Almost dropping the wine, she twisted her body, slipping and falling into the tub with a splash.

As she held the bottle over her head, he took it from her and smiled. "You didn't even spill a drop. Thank you."

"Look what ye did!" she shouted.

"Shhh." He held a finger to her lips and glanced back at the door. "We wouldn't want anyone to hear us."

"Look what ye did," she said in a hoarse whisper.

"Me?" He had the audacity to laugh at her. "I did nothing. That was all you."

Having fallen over his lap, Morag put her hand into the water to push herself up. But when she did, she accidentally touched his erection.

"Keep that up and we'll be making love in the water before you have a chance to scream again."

She was about to protest to his absurd suggestion, but when he brushed back a lock of her wet hair and gazed into her eyes, her actions stilled. And when he leaned over and kissed her, she felt her body tremble with excitement and anticipation. Morag knew it was wrong to make love with a man before they were married. But they were betrothed and Lady Ernestine said they'd be married before she chose the earl's successor. That was only a sennight away. Mayhap, it didn't matter after all.

"Kiss me again," she said, but he didn't. Instead, he took a swig of wine and let out a deep breath.

"Morag, there is something I've been meaning to talk to you about."

"Give me some wine," she said, grabbing the bottle and chugging some down, trying to calm her nerves. If she was going to do this, she needed to be relaxed so it wouldn't hurt.

She had ears and heard from her sister and cousins what it was like to be bedded by a man. They said it might hurt the first time but afterwards it was very pleasurable, indeed. She wanted to feel that same pleasure.

"Slow down," he said, taking the bottle from her, reaching back and placing it on the floor. "You keep that up and you're going to do something you'll regret."

"Nay, I'll never regret anythin' that has to do with lovin' ye." She brashly reached up and pulled Bedivere's face to hers and kissed him passionately, using her tongue the way she heard pleased a man. She wanted to pleasure her future husband now, and later after the wedding as well.

"Stop it, Morag. I am trying to talk to you." He pushed her away and she didn't understand his actions.

"What's the matter?" she asked, wondering if she had done something wrong.

"We can't do this."

"Why no'?"

"Because it's not right."

"Ah, ye're right. I see the problem."

It pained Bedivere to have to push Morag away when he wanted her so badly. Still, he couldn't take her virginity under false pretenses. He didn't plan on going through with the wedding, even if he did have feelings for her. He had to tell her the truth about him, and that is just what he planned to do.

But then the little Vixen surprised him once again. Right when he thought she was getting out of the tub, she stood up and started untying the laces of her bodice, looking at him in lust.

"M-Morag. What are you doing?"

"I ken why ye said we couldna make love like this. It's because I need to remove my clothes first."

"Nay, that's not what I meant." He held out his hand to stop her, but she plopped down her bodice over his arm and, in one motion, lifted her tunic over her head.

"What did ye mean, then?" she asked, standing in the tub half-naked.

He couldn't answer because his eyes were fastened to her perky bare breasts with her nipples standing at attention like soldiers. All sense left his head and it was as if he had forgotten how to speak.

"I – I." His manhood stiffened more, sticking up out of the water. There was no way he could tell her he didn't want her now and have her believe it. Her hooded eyes lowered to the evidence of his arousal.

"I want to do this right for my future husband." She dropped her skirt and braies, throwing them over the side of the tub toward the raging fire with a slosh of water. Standing in front of him naked as the day she was born, Bedivere thought she was the prettiest girl he had ever seen in his life. Then she seemed to suddenly get shy under his perusal. Crossing her arms over her chest to hide her nakedness, the smile left her face and she glanced over at the hearth.

"You are beautiful," he said in a breathy whisper. Shyly, she shifted her glance toward him and lowered herself down into the water. "You want this, don't you?" he asked.

"Aye. I want to make love with ye and ken how it feels to be brought to completion. I want to feel sated and be able to satisfy ye, too."

"But it's not right, Morag. You are a virgin, are you not?"

"Aye. And I am also eight and ten years of age and afeared I will never experience what other lassies my age have already kent for years."

"I don't know, Morag." His head told him not to couple with her but his heart told him to do it.

"Dinna ye want to make love with me?" she asked, putting up her protective wall by hiding her breasts with her arms.

"I do," he said, reaching out and running his hand along the side of her face. "But I don't want to do it until –"

"Until we're married," she finished his sentence for him. "It's all right, Bedivere. We are betrothed and will be married within a week's time."

"But you don't even know me," he said, trying to start a conversation with her about who he really was.

"I was hopin' to get to ken ye better. That's why I'm here."

"Morag, you need to know that I'm not who you think I am." There, he said it. This should open up the conversation and he could tell her what he did for a living.

"I am no' who ye think I am either."

"You're not?" He raised an eyebrow, wondering what she meant.

"I ken right now ye think I am a strumpet, but I assure ye that I am no'."

"Nay, I don't think that at all."

"I am only actin' this way because I'm afeared."

"Afraid? I don't understand," he said.

"I've always been left out of everythin' my entire life," she told him.

"I didn't know that." His heart went out to her when he saw her brush away a tear with the back of her hand.

"My sister and cousins were chosen, but I wasna. They got

crowns, but I didna. I wasna important enough, and they never wanted me around."

"Chosen?" he asked curiously. "For what? And why do they have crowns?"

"I am sorry, but I canna tell ye."

Bedivere shook his head and chuckled. "Morag, you make no sense."

"I have some secrets, Bedivere. Secrets that I canna tell even ye."

"Secrets," he repeated, thinking this was the perfect time to come clean about his past. "We all have secrets, Morag. There is nothing wrong with that."

She trembled and he pulled her closer to him to comfort her.

"But my secrets are big. And ye, who are about to be my husband, might no' like them."

"Why don't you tell them to me?"

"I would if I could, but I promised no' to say a word."

"You did?" He found it amusing that the queen of gossip was refusing to talk.

"If you tell me your secrets, I'll tell you mine." That should arouse her curiosity.

"I dinna care if ye have secrets," she said, surprising him to no end. "I still want to marry ye and be yer wife."

"You can't mean that." He pulled her against his chest and smoothed back her hair.

"I have been kent to be a gossip my entire life, and I'm tired of it," she told him. "Recently, someone told me to use my gossipin' for guid, but I dinna understand how I can possibly do that." She looked up to him with wide, glassy eyes. "Do ye?"

"Nay," he said, with a shake of his head. "I can't say I know how to use gossip for good, but I assure you if I think of something, I will let you know."

"Guid," she said. "Will ye make love to me now?"

"Not before I tell you a little about myself. You see, I am not the kind, generous, protective, chivalric man you think me to be."

"Ye are bein' modest just like ye said my uncles were bein' when they turned down the invitation to compete for the earl's holdin's."

"I assure you, it has nothing to do with modesty."

"Ye are no' goin' to turn me away, are ye, Bedivere?"

She looked so sad that it about broke his heart. "Well I —"

"I dinna want ye to ever forget me."

"Nay, I promise I won't."

"Ye're goin' to leave me. I can tell." Her body became tense and she seemed to panic.

"It's not that I'm going to leave you, Morag. It's just that with my past, I don't think you'd want to be married to me."

"Leave the past in the past and live in the now," she told him. "If no', there will never be a chance for a future between us."

"What are you saying? That you don't want me to tell you anything about myself?"

"Nay. I am just sayin' that I dinna care who ye were in the past. All I care about is who ye are now." With that, she reached up and kissed him hungrily, climbing atop his lap.

Morag's words were like music to his ears. If she truly didn't care about his past, then she honestly was the angel he thought her to be. He needed a new life, and wanted one desperately. And with Morag at his side, he felt as if he had hope again for the first time. Mayhap, with her light, the darkness of his blackened soul could be purged after all. If she could truly accept him for who he was, then that was all that mattered.

In heated passion, they kissed and all thoughts of breaking the betrothal left his mind. He ran his hands down her back, feeling her quiver under his touch.

"I want ye, Bedivere," she whispered, throwing back her head, letting her long hair float on the surface of the water. She looked like a siren, if there were such things. Her body was warm and pressed up against him, making his lust for her out of control. He had to have her.

"I want you, too, Morag," he said between kisses. "I want you more than I've ever wanted a woman in my life." His kisses trailed to her chest and his lips closed over one hardened nipple. Using his tongue, he swirled it around her nub causing her to moan slightly. Then to his surprise, she reached down and touched him under the water.

He groaned, trying to hold back, feeling as if he were about to burst. With both hands, he cupped her buttocks and spread her legs, bringing her over him, slowly sliding her down his hardened shaft.

"Och, we are doin' it," she cried out in excitement. Her innocence was like a breath of fresh air in his murky life. "I like it," she told him. "It doesna hurt at all."

"It gets even better," he assured her. "But it is too cramped in here for me to pleasure you properly. I am going to take you to my bed."

In one motion, he picked her up, her legs still spread around his waist. She giggled and held on to his shoulders.

"Dinna drop me," she said as he stepped from the tub, spilling water all over the rushes on the floor.

"I would never drop you," he said, kissing the side of her neck as he brought her to the bed. Still holding on to her, he pulled back the blanket and laid her atop the sheets. "I think I am falling in love with you, Morag."

"Bedivere, I feel the same way about ye."

"I have never met anyone like you. You are special. You are my saving grace. My angel."

Morag loved the way her future husband spoke about her. Never in her life had she felt as loved as she did right now. At first, she wondered if she was being too bold by coming here tonight. But now, she was sure she hadn't made a mistake after all.

"Is there more?" she asked, curious to experience everything, not really sure if they had completed the act or not.

"There is plenty more. Now, let me pleasure you."

With that, he trailed kisses down her chest and suckled at her, causing her back to arch as her body became alive beneath him. He was gentle and caring. And when he entered her again, he took his time, letting her get accustomed to his size.

She felt his length inside her, and it excited her and made her want more. Her body vibrated and when he moved his hips to thrust, she followed his actions and raised her legs up around his waist, gripping at his hair as he slid in and out.

Something happened then that she wasn't expecting. She felt her womanhood come to life and it was the best feeling she had ever known. Crying out in elation, she and Bedivere did the dance of love.

Her world exploded behind her closed lids and she felt loved, truly loved for the first time in her life. Then, with a few grunts and groans of lovemaking, Bedivere released his passion within her as he met his peak. Together, they held each other, not letting go at all as they fell asleep in each other's arms.

CHAPTER 12

Morag awoke before Bedivere the next morning, feeling happy and sated. Last night was wonderful and she didn't want her intimate time with her future husband to ever end. Finally, she'd found what she'd been looking for in life. With Bedivere, Morag felt wanted and loved. With him, she would never feel left out of anything again.

Lying next to him, she took a minute to study the lines of his face and the way his bushy eyebrows turned down slightly at the corners when he slept. The morning light filtering in through the shutter made a streak across his face and bare, broad chest. He always looked handsome, but without the beard and mustache he was even more desirable. She leaned in and very gently placed a small kiss against his lips. He made a small noise and turned over in bed.

Being careful not to wake him, Morag tiptoed over to the dying fire to stoke it. As the flames reignited, she felt her clothes. They were still wet, but she donned them anyway. Feeling cold, she reached for the blanket on the floor. When she picked it up, there was a loud clattering of metal as objects that were hidden inside the folded blanket fell to the floor at her feet.

"What's this?" she asked, reaching down to pick up one of the many blades. There were at least a dozen weapons – daggers, swords, and some that she couldn't even identify.

"Nay, put those down!" Bedivere shot off the bed, still naked, and reached out and took the dagger from her.

"What are all these weapons?" she asked.

"They . . . they're mine."

"But why do ye have so many? What do ye use them for?"

"I'm a knight. Of course I have weapons."

She looked at him from the corners of her eyes. "Bedivere, I dinna understand."

"Morag, I tried to tell you things about me last night. But you said you didn't want to hear my secrets and that they didn't matter."

"Secrets? What kind of secrets?" she asked, looking down to the weapons. Her stomach clenched. Bedivere was hiding something from her and she had a feeling that whatever it was she wasn't going to like it.

"Brother, I've returned." Percival burst into the room with another man right behind him. "Oh!" Percival stepped backward, crashing into the other man, holding his hand up to his eyes. "Sorry, I didn't know you had a . . . visitor."

"Did ye call him, Brother?" asked Morag, not understanding this at all. "Bedivere, I thought he was yer squire."

Bedivere put down the dagger and hurriedly dressed. "Dammit, Percival, why can't you knock like a normal person before entering my chamber?"

"Perhaps we should come back at a . . . more convenient time?" asked the other man.

"No need. I am leavin'." Morag hurried for the door, wanting nothing more than to leave since she felt embarrassed being caught in Bedivere's room.

"Morag, wait!" Bedivere called after her. "I can explain."

"Explain? What are you saying?" growled the other visitor.

"God's eyes, Whitmore, I think she has the right to know that Percival is my brother." Bedivere walked over to Morag, barechested and with bare feet but wearing breeches. He took Morag by the wrist. "I need to talk with you," he said in a low voice.

"Nay," said Morag, feeling betrayed by her lover. "I dinna have anythin' to say to ye."

"Meet me in the mews in an hour," he whispered as he gently kissed her ear.

"Let go of me," she snapped, running past Percival and the man called Whitmore, feeling as if, mayhap, she had done wrong by sleeping with Bedivere after all.

"WHAT WAS THAT ALL ABOUT, BEDIVERE?" asked Lord Whitmore as he entered the room and closed the door behind him.

"What the hell are you doing here?" Bedivere growled, pulling a tunic over his head.

"I gave him your message, just like you told me to do," said Percival. "He insisted on coming here to talk to you himself."

"I have nothing to talk about with him." Bedivere sat on a chair to put on his shoes.

Whitmore chuckled. "Now you are starting to sound just like that tart you bedded."

Bedivere shot up off the bed, grabbing Lord John Whitmore by the front of his tunic and pushing his face close to the man's. "You call her a tart once more and I'll kill you right where you stand. And I think you know better than anyone that I'm capable of doing it."

"Bedivere, don't," warned Percival in concern.

"That's right," said Whitmore. "Unless you've forgotten, I still hold your mother captive. And if anything happens to me, I have given my men orders to kill your mother and to hunt you down as well."

"Let him go," begged Percival.

Bedivere's blood boiled and he wanted to kill Whitmore more than he ever had before. It was this man who had made his life a living hell. It was he who killed his father and imprisoned his family. Aye, Lord John Whitmore was a man who Bedivere hated with every fiber of his being.

"Damn you!" he growled, releasing Whitmore with a push. "Why are you even here? It's much too risky."

"Especially with the daughter of one of the Legendary Bastards of the Crown in your bed. Now I understand why you refused your orders." Whitmore walked over to the table and inspected the bottle for leftover wine.

"We had a deal. One for one," Bedivere reminded him. "I am not, and will not take on all three of the bastards."

"They are conspiring to kill King Richard." Whitmore put down the empty wine bottle and ran his finger over the rim. "They have to go."

"Then do it yourself."

"You owe me one last job!"

Bedivere's head snapped up because Whitmore made it

sound as if he owed only him. "Don't you mean I owe you and the king both?"

"Aye, that's what I meant."

"So be it. I'll give you one more, but one only. And it won't be those three."

"Nay, it won't."

Bedivere turned back toward him, curious as to what he meant. "How so?"

"You don't have to worry about taking out all three. I've already given the order to two other trained killers who will handle that."

"Who? Who did you send to do your dirty work? I want to know." Bedivere's hands balled up into fists.

Whitmore chuckled. "Now, now, Bedivere. You know it doesn't work that way. Their identities will remain anonymous. Only I know who they are. All you have to worry about is the last one."

"Last one? What do you mean?"

"Your mark. The girl's father."

Upon hearing this, Bedivere's teeth gnashed together so hard that he felt the tension in his jaw. "Don't do this to me," he said. "Haven't I gone through enough already?"

"It's for the crown," said Whitmore, heading toward the door. "Would you question your orders from your king?"

"Nay. Of course not," Bedivere mumbled. "But there must be another way."

"You will do as you're told, or you'll never see your mother again." Whitmore stopped with his hand on the door latch. "Oh, and don't even think of warning the bastard triplets because if you do, that wench that warmed your bed will die."

"You son of a jackal!" spat Bedivere. "You harm a hair on Morag's head and I will personally make you pay."

"Don't forget who you're talking to," warned the man. "And also don't forget who holds the life of your mother on a very delicate thread." He chuckled again and left the room, closing the door behind him.

"Damn you!" cried Bedivere, picking up the wine bottle and hurling it at the door. It smashed against the wood and fell to the floor.

"Brother, what are you going to do?" asked Percival.

"Me? You mean we." Bedivere paced back and forth.

"Oh no. Not me. I am not going to kill anyone."

"Percival, stop it." Bedivere stopped pacing and stared at his brother. "You are the son of a knight and even if you've never killed a man, it is time you go to battle. Start acting like the man Father wanted you to be."

"I don't think Father would have looked kindly on your profession." Percival nodded to the blades scattered across the floor.

"I didn't have a choice. I took on the responsibility to clean up the mess that Father left. If you think badly of me for my decision, then so be it. I don't care."

"Nay, of course I don't." Percival hung his head. "I admire you for your strength, Brother. If there's anything you need to me do . . . then I will do it."

"Good." Bedivere walked over and put his arm around his brother's shoulders. He looked back to the door and spoke softly. "I need you to get our aunt and uncle and our siblings."

Percival looked at him in surprise. "They are already with the villagers in hiding, like you told me."

"Then get them out of hiding and bring them here to Rothbury."

"Here?" Percival shook his head in confusion. "I don't understand. Whitmore will see them."

"Aye, I hope he does. Anything that makes him uncomfortable will help as a distraction."

"Distraction? From what?"

"Didn't you hear him? There are two other assassins within Rothbury's walls. I need to figure out who they are and stop them before they try to attack Morag's uncles."

"Won't our family be in danger here?"

"I have a plan that will make them safe. We'll keep them in plain view and close to Lady Ernestine. Go now, and bring them back quickly. And don't say a word of what happened to our family to anyone. Do you understand me?"

"Aye, but what about Mother?"

"I'm working on that."

"You're not really going to kill Morag's father, are you?"

"Morag," he said under his breath, thinking about their intimate time together. "I'm afraid I've made a mess of things and need to find her right away and fix it."

"You're not going to tell her any of this, are you?"

Bedivere strapped on his weapon belt and headed for the door. "I don't know what I'm going to do yet, but I hope to figure it out fast or I'm going to lose her forever."

CHAPTER 13

*M*orag rode as fast as she could to the secret garden, tears streaming down her face. Bedivere had lied to her and she couldn't figure out why. She needed to talk to someone, and since her sister and cousins were no longer here, the only one she could trust was Mazelina.

"Mazelina, I need ye," she cried, rushing into the garden, leaving the gate open and not bothering to tie the reins of the horse to a tree. "Mazelina, where are ye?"

She rushed up the stairs and into the cottage. When there was no sign of the old woman anywhere, she went to the stable and then the shed. Not finding her, she scanned the garden once more but there was no sign of life.

Feeling scared and all alone, Morag ran to the grave of Imanie and fell to her knees. "Oh, Imanie, where are ye when I need ye?" She put her head down on the ground and wept bitterly.

"Morag, I'm here."

Morag's head sprang up to see Mazelina on the porch of

the house. Morag got up and picked up her skirts and ran to the woman. Just as she was about to throw herself into Mazelina's arms, the old woman stopped her with a halting hand in the air.

"Enough. Go in the house and we'll talk."

Morag opened the door, holding it for the old woman and followed her inside. Once in there, she sank down atop the wooden bench at the table.

"Oh, Mazelina, I think I made a terrible mistake."

"Did you put your heart before your head?"

"Aye, I did. I coupled with Bedivere and now I think, mayhap, I shouldna have."

"What made you change your mind?"

"I didna think it was wrong since we were betrothed but, mayhap, I should have waited."

"Really?"

"Aye, because now I dinna ken if I want to marry him anymore."

"Why not?"

Morag looked up, telling Mazelina everything. "He had dozens of weapons hidden in a blanket, and told me he has secrets of his past. He lied to me and told me Percival was his squire but I heard Percival call him Brother. Percival almost caught me naked when he burst into the bedchamber with a man name Lord Whitmore."

"Whitmore?" asked Mazelina. "Morag, you should stay away from that man."

"Bedivere didna tell me the truth. He kept things from me and now I dinna ken if I can trust him."

"And you didn't keep secrets from him as well?"

"Of course, I did. I am sworn to secrecy about ye and about bein' a member of the Followers of the Secret Heart."

"How do you know he isn't sworn to secrecy about something as well?"

"I dinna like secrets."

"Everyone knows that."

"He deceived me by keepin' things from me. Things that I still dinna ken but I feel it is somethin' bad."

"You told him you didn't want to know his secrets about his past, so was he really doing anything wrong?"

"I didna."

"You did." Mazelina crossed her arms over her chest and scowled at Morag.

"Aye, I suppose I did." She sniffed and used a cloth from her pocket to dab at her tears. "I keep forgettin' ye can read minds."

"So what are you going to do?"

"Me?" She looked up with wide eyes and then narrowed her eyes as she thought of Bedivere and became angry. "I'm no' goin' to speak to him ever again."

"Mayhap, not communicating is what got you into this bind to begin with."

"What should I do?" asked Morag, looking for guidance.

"Be strong, Morag. The Followers of the Secret Heart is a group only for strong women."

"That's why I wasna asked to be in it." She sadly rested her head in her arms on the table. "I am no' strong like Fia or Willow and Maira. I wish they were here right now to help me."

"You are strong, Morag, but you need to take control of your life and stop living the same way you did as a child."

"I dinna understand."

"When you were a child, you were a follower. You always looked to others for your answers as well as for your strength. You don't need me to guide you, Morag. I think my presence here is only making you rely on someone else instead of yourself."

"Nay, dinna say that," cried Morag, feeling it in the pit of her stomach that Mazelina was about to leave her. "Everyone leaves me. Dinna go. Please, stay," she begged her. "I need ye. Dinna abandon me like everyone else."

"Stop playing the victim and pick up your chin proudly and have faith in yourself."

Tears streamed from Morag's eyes. What she needed now was comforting but all she got were a few cold words that slapped her like a hand across her face. The sound of her horse whinnying caused her to jump up and run to the door. When she looked out, she saw the back end of it leaving through the gate of the secret garden. She had been in such a hurry to get to Mazelina and so upset by Bedivere, that she had neglected to tie it up properly.

"Nay!" she cried, taking a step out the door and then turning back around to talk to Mazelina. "Dinna leave. I'll be right back."

"I won't be here when you return, Morag."

That upset Morag and she bit her lip to keep from crying, shaking her head. "Then ye really are goin' to abandon me just like everyone else?"

"Is that what you think they all did?"

A flash of lightning and a clap of thunder filled the sky making Morag jump. She needed to go after her horse but was afraid if she left Mazelina, she would never see the woman again. "I'm no' done with my trainin' yet," she told her. "Ye canna leave me before I have learned to master my skill and do great things like the others."

"Only you can decide if you will do great things or not in life. No mentor can teach you anything that, deep down, you don't already know. The wisdom to guide you is already within you, and has been there all the time. Now, you just need to believe it. You need to believe in yourself."

"Do ye believe in me?" asked Morag. "Do ye really think I can do great things?"

"It doesn't matter what anyone else thinks. Your decisions are yours alone. Now go, and look inside yourself and make the choices that feel right."

"But how will I ken?"

"You'll know." The woman smiled and nodded and held her hand to her heart. "After all, you are a member of the Followers of the Secret Heart, so listen to your heart."

"Thank ye," said Morag, taking her last look at the old woman that she would never see again. Then, taking a deep breath, she looked out to the secret garden as the sky opened and the rain pelted down. She could stay here until after the storm but, if so, she may never find her horse. Bandits could claim it by then. There was no one here to help her and she had to trust in herself. She needed to be brave. She had to go.

Releasing her breath, she lifted her hood and stepped out in the pouring rain, ready to take control of her destiny for the first time in her life.

BEDIVERE RODE his horse through the forest in the rain,

looking for Morag. When he discovered her horse missing from the stable, he figured she had come to the secret garden again. A horrible, threatening storm stirred all around him, and he was half-tempted to go back to the castle, but he didn't. Morag was out here somewhere and he had to find her. She was most likely alone and possibly in danger.

Now that Whitmore had arrived at the castle, no one was safe. Any turn of events and the vile man could command one of the secret assassins to kill Morag or any one of them.

"Morag," he called out, using his hand as a shield from the rain, sure he saw something move up ahead. His hand went to his sword as he rode forward. Then he saw it. Morag's horse was pulling at its reins that were caught on a branch of a tree.

He rode up and untangled the reins, tying the horse to his horse's saddle. "Morag," he called out once again, his eyes scanning the area. He didn't see her anywhere and couldn't seem to find the gate of the secret garden. He cursed under his breath, now regretting not telling her the truth about him. She knew he'd kept things from her and he wasn't sure she didn't hate him at this moment.

He'd claimed the girl's innocence last night and now regretted his actions. Never should he have taken her to his bed. In a moment of weakness, he let down his guard, feeling carefree and happy again. He hadn't felt that way in years now, but was it worth it? For one night of pleasure, he had ruined anything that had developed between them.

"Bedivere?" He heard a faint voice and looked up to see Morag trudging through the forest on foot. Lightning flashed again and he felt the hair on his arms rise. A loud cracking sound up in the canopy made him realize lightning had struck a limb of a tree and it was right above Morag.

"Morag!" he shouted, racing forward on his horse, reaching down and scooping her up just as a large limb fell to the ground, crashing down right next to them. Morag's horse became skittish and reared up, pulling at the reins. "Hold on to me," he commanded, trying to hold back his own horse from running, while reaching back for the reins of Morag's horse and trying to calm it at the same time.

"Bedivere, I'm scared," said Morag, her arms wrapped around his waist as she sat in front of him. He managed to take control of the horses and headed back to the castle in the pouring rain.

"Don't be frightened," he told her. "As long as you're with me, I will protect you. Do not worry."

"I'm no' frightened anymore now that I'm with ye," she told him. "But I am still angry with ye, I must admit."

"I know. And rightly so," he agreed, holding to her tightly, never wanting to let her go. "We need to talk, Morag. There are some things I need to tell you, and they can no longer wait."

CHAPTER 14

*B*edivere had decided to tell Morag about his past, and would have done so if all hell hadn't broken loose as soon as they returned to the castle.

"Fire!" someone shouted, causing Bedivere to look up to find that lightning had hit the mews and it was going up in flame. Everyone rushed back and forth with buckets, bringing water from the well. He dismounted and helped Morag from her horse, knowing he had to help.

"Go to your chamber and keep dry. Stay there and don't open the door for anyone until I arrive."

"I will no'!" she said stubbornly. "I am goin' to help save the mews as well."

"Bedivere, hurry!" It was Percival, coming out of the mews with a hawk on his arm. The bird flapped its wings wildly, frightened and trying to get away but secured to his arm by the jess. He held a large cage in his other hand.

"Give me the cage," said Morag, taking it and opening the door and guiding the bird inside. "We need to go quickly and get the rest of the birds before they die." Morag took off at a run for the burning mews with Percival right behind her.

"Morag, wait! Don't go in there. It's dangerous," cried Bedivere, taking two buckets of water from a servant.

"Let her go. It'll save you a lot of trouble later if she perishes in the fire." Whitmore stood nearby watching, doing nothing to help.

"Get the hell out of my sight," Bedivere growled, heading for the mews with the water.

MORAG COUGHED, covering her face with her arm as she helped Percival and Lady Ernestine try to save the birds in the mews. She thought naught of herself, but rather for the poor animals that were about to lose their lives because of an act of nature.

"Morag, get out of here." Bedivere flung the water from the buckets at the flames. Before she could even answer, a burning beam fell from the roof, about to hit Lady Ernestine.

"Lady Rothbury, watch out," cried Morag, causing the woman to look up and move out of the way. However, she was hit in the shoulder and fell to the ground. Then to Morag's horror, the woman's gown caught afire.

"Nay!" cried Morag, starting toward her.

"I've got her." Bedivere shot forward, removing his cloak and using it to smother the flames on her gown. Then he picked up Lady Ernestine in his arms. "Everyone out of here now," he shouted, looking upward. "The roof is going to cave in."

Picking up a frightened falcon, Morag followed Percival as

they ran from the mews. Just as Bedivere exited carrying Lady Ernestine, the building collapsed behind them.

"Lady Ernestine!" Morag ran to the woman who clung to Bedivere. The shoulder of her gown was torn and Morag noticed that she was scratched. The bottom of her gown was burned.

"Sir Bedivere, you saved my life," said the lady of the castle.

"Bring her inside at once and I'll find the healer," said Morag, looking back to the mews. There was nothing they could do to save it now. The rain fell harder, helping to douse the flames, but causing the building to smolder.

"We did all we could to save it," said Bedivere. "The rain will put out the rest of the fire."

"I've got the birds," shouted Percival, heading into the great hall with the cage.

"Thank ye," said Morag to Bedivere. He had first saved her and now Lady Ernestine. She felt it in her heart, that no matter what his dark secret was, he was still a good man.

"I think I see the healer near the front gate. I will send him to the great hall immediately." Morag picked up her soggy skirts and ran to the front gate. "Healer, Lady Ernestine is wounded and needs your help."

When the man turned around, she realized that, although he wore the healer's cloak, she didn't recognize him.

"Oh, I'm sorry. I thought ye were someone else. I am lookin' for the healer."

"He had a call in the village but I am here to take his place," said the man.

"Thank ye. Please go to the great hall and help Lady Ernestine at once."

"Aye, my lady," said the man with a bow, heading away with a travel bag slung over his shoulder. She looked down to see his feet, surprised he wore muddy boots instead of shoes. He also had a very sharp dagger hanging at his side. It seemed odd but she hadn't a moment to think about it before she heard someone calling her name.

"Morag! Morag, over here."

"Willow?" asked Morag, squinting her eyes to see through the rain. Her cousin rode in a horse-drawn cart driven by a servant. She was escorted by her father, who led the way over the drawbridge. "Uncle Rook!" Morag ran to greet them, happy to have some of her family here at last. "Where are Sir Conrad and Aunt Calliope?" she asked, inquiring about Willow's husband and Rook's wife.

"We came alone," said Willow. "They were not able to make it. Once we got the missive saying you signed my father up for the competition, we knew we had to be here."

"What's going on over there?" Rook slid off his horse and threw the reins to a stable boy, eyeing up the smoldering mews.

"Lightnin' struck the mews and Lady Ernestine was injured," Morag explained.

Rook removed his cloak and threw it in the cart. After helping his pregnant daughter to the ground, he took off at a run to help with the burning mews.

"Willow, I'm so happy ye are here." Morag fell into her cousin's embrace. "My, ye are gettin' big," she said, rubbing Willow's belly.

"I'm not big, I'm six month's pregnant," Willow answered with a sniff. "Morag, I need to get out of the rain and this smoke. It's not good for the baby."

Morag looked over to the mews, seeing that the situation was being handled. "Let's go to my chamber and change into dry clothes. Then I want to check on Lady Ernestine."

Willow and Morag entered the keep, stopping at the door to the great hall where Bedivere was tending to Lady Ernestine. He looked up anxiously and summoned her with a wave of his hand.

"Is that Sir Bedivere Hamilton?" asked Willow.

"Aye," said Morag, smiling at Bedivere, proud of what he had done. "We are betrothed."

"Betrothed?" Willow held a look of horror on her face. "Nay, Morag, you can't be."

"Well, we are. Now give me a moment to see what Bedivere wants and I'll meet ye up in my chamber."

"Where do you want the trunk?" asked Willow's servant, hauling it into the keep.

"It's the first room up the stairs on the right," Morag told the boy and ran to Bedivere's side.

"Where is the healer?" growled Bedivere. "I thought you were going to send him over."

"He's no' here?" She looked around. "I was told the castle's healer was in the village and that another healer is takin' his place. I sent him over here. I wonder where he is."

"Nonsense, I don't need a healer." Lady Ernestine called to her handmaid. "All I need is to wash up and change and I will be right back to check on the situation. Sir Bedivere, would you be kind enough to see that things are in order at the mews?"

"Of course, my lady," he said with a bow.

"My Uncle Rook is out there, too," Morag told him.

Bedivere's head snapped up. "Sir Rook is here?"

"Aye," she told him. "He just arrived with my cousin, Willow."

"Morag, come here," called out Willow impatiently.

"I'd better go. Willow is pregnant and wet and that is never a good combination."

"Morag, wait." Bedivere followed her and stopped her with a hand to the shoulder.

"What is it?" she asked.

He looked over her head at Willow, and seemed disturbed. "I have been trying to talk to you."

"We'll talk, I promise." She reached up and kissed him on his cheek. "Right after I see to my cousin and ye see to the mews." She hurried over to Willow and they ascended the stairs. As soon as they entered the room, the servant left and closed the door. Willow grabbed Morag's hand.

"Sit down," said Willow, seeming very upset for some reason.

"Sit down?" Morag looked at her as if she were addled. "We are soppin' wet. We need to remove our clothes and dry ourselves by the fire." Morag turned to go to the hearth.

"You can't marry Bedivere," Willow blurted out, stopping Morag in her tracks.

"Why no'?" she asked her cousin.

"Because, he is not who you think he is."

Morag smiled. "He is a wonderful, carin' man who I ken will always protect me."

"He's got a secret, Morag," said Willow with urgency in her voice. "It is a very dark secret."

"Secret?" Morag turned back to the hearth and warmed her hands at the fire. "We all have secrets, Cousin."

"Not like this one."

Suddenly, Morag wondered what Bedivere had been trying to tell her. Hadn't he said last night that he was harboring secrets and she told him she didn't care? Now, she wondered if she should have let him explain before things went so far.

"I dinna care and dinna want to ken," she said, not wanting anything to ruin her plans for the future with Bedivere. She tried to convince herself that she didn't want to hear it, but something still ate away at her about his secrecy. Morag couldn't ignore it, she had to know. Still, part of her tried hard not to gossip.

"All right, then," said Willow. "If you want to marry a man that you know nothing about, then so be it."

Morag turned to see Willow removing her cloak and settling herself on the bed. "How do ye ken his secret and I dinna?"

"I found out when I was searching for the thief who stole the ruby."

"So . . . is he a thief, then?"

"Nay. I wish that was all it was." Willow kicked off her shoes.

Her cousin's comment made Morag curious. It was driving her mad and she just had to know. Her desire to gossip and hear gossip got the best of her at last. Turning on her heel, she headed over to the bed and plopped down in her wet clothes next to her cousin. "All right. Tell me what ye ken about my betrothed."

"I thought you said you didn't care and didn't want to know." Willow shot her a sly smile.

"Well, I've changed my mind."

"I knew you would." Willow reached out to put her arm around Morag's shoulders but then pulled back and made a face because her clothes and hair was soaking wet.

"Tell me, Willow!" Morag grabbed Willow's hand. "I have to ken."

"All right, I'll tell you even though I promised I wouldn't tell a soul. But it's only because you need to know the truth before your relationship with him goes too far."

"Willow, what is it?" Morag's head dizzied and her heart sped up. The last thing she wanted to hear about Bedivere was something bad. After giving her heart to the man and losing her virginity to him as well, she didn't want anything to ruin her plans for the future.

"He's . . . he's an assassin, Morag." Willow looked directly into her eyes when she spoke and there was no doubt that she told the truth.

Morag's jaw dropped open. Now it made sense why Bedivere had so many weapons hidden in his room. How could Morag be so blind?

"An assassin?" she asked, hoping she had heard her cousin wrong.

"Aye. You need to distance yourself from him right now, and break the betrothal. If not, when your father finds out, he's going to kill Bedivere."

"Oh, Willow," said Morag, squeezing her cousin's hand. "I canna break the betrothal." A feeling of panic engulfed her.

"Of course, you can. You aren't married yet, so it isn't too late. Plus, your father never agreed to the marriage in the first place, so you have no choice but to do it."

"Och, Willow, I have put myself in a verra terrible position."

"What are you talking about?" Willow peered at Morag from the sides of her eyes. "Morag . . . what did you do?"

"I canna break the betrothal because it is too late," Morag admitted. "Sir Bedivere and I have already coupled."

CHAPTER 15

By the time Bedivere helped settle things at the mews, helped clean up, and checked on Lady Ernestine, it was late in the day. He was wet and exhausted, and hadn't had a moment to himself to look for Morag.

"Bedivere, you saved Lady Ernestine's life," said Percival, tending to the birds that had been saved from the fire. He let the birds fly free in the great hall, but took special care of those that were injured.

"I suppose I did," he mumbled, having too much on his mind to bask in the glory of one heroic act. He'd been keeping an eye on Whitmore all night, and also surveying every man that walked by wondering which two were the assassins sent to kill the bastards of the crown. Now that Lord Rook was here, the situation was even more dire. He had to keep an ear and eye on him at all times. He wasn't about to let the triplets be killed.

"Sir Bedivere," said Lord Rook, following him into the keep. "We meet again."

"Aye," he said with a nod of his head, not sure if Willow

had told him his secret. He supposed if she had, he wouldn't be smiling.

"Sorry that my daughter declined your offer of marriage. She and Sir Conrad are happily married and having their first baby in a few months' time."

"Aye, that's nice." Bedivere couldn't care less.

"Well, since I'm here, how about if we share an ale together at the fire while we warm our bones and dry our clothes."

"Of course." Bedivere looked over his shoulder, watching for Morag. He hadn't yet had a private moment to talk to her and now that Willow was here, she was sure to expose him. "Do you have a place to stay while you're here?"

"I suppose I'll sleep in the great hall," answered Rook. "I believe Willow will be sharing Morag's chamber."

"Nay, you can't stay here." Bedivere peered across the hall to see Whitmore watching them intently. Suddenly, every man looked suspicious to Bedivere and he felt like he wouldn't get a good sleep unless he could protect Lord Rook by knowing where he was at all times. "You'll stay with me in my solar."

"That's kind of you, but not necessary," answered Rook, scooping two tankards of ale off a serving wench's tray and handing one to Bedivere.

"Really, I insist." Bedivere took a long draw of ale, his eyes never leaving Rook.

"Well, all right, then," said Rook. "I would be a fool to turn down such an offer."

Bedivere let out a sigh of relief. "Why don't we finish this drink up in my chamber so I can get into dry clothes and rid myself of this chill."

"Of course," said Rook, following Bedivere across the great hall.

Bedivere stopped for only a moment on his way upstairs to whisper to his brother. "Plans have changed. Leave the family where they are and, instead, keep an eye out for anyone that looks suspicious."

Percival jerked backward when he saw Rook. "Aren't you one of the Legendary Bastards of the Crown?" he asked him.

"Aye," chuckled Rook. "You might know me as Rook the Ruthless, although I can't say I am that ruthless anymore. What is your name?"

"Percival," he answered. "I'm Bedivere's . . . squire," he said, looking down to the floor.

"Actually, Percival is my younger brother," said Bedivere, not wanting to lie any more than he had to. Percival's face lit up when Bedivere referred to him as family.

"I see the resemblance," said Rook. "Won't you join us in the solar for an ale as well?"

"Aye," said Percival at the same time Bedivere said, "nay."

"My brother has a lot to do." Bedivere motioned with his eyes for Percival to leave.

"Nay, I don't," said Percival.

"I thought you were going to keep your eye on things," Bedivere told him, stressing the words things. "That is, with the birds flying loose and all," he added so Rook wouldn't get suspicious.

"Oh, I am." Percival sounded disappointed, but turned and headed back into the great hall.

"This way, Sir Rook," said Bedivere, leading the man who he'd been commissioned to kill up to his room.

* * *

Morag jumped off the bed when the door opened, wiping the tears from her eyes and faking a smile.

"Thank you," Willow told the servant, taking the food from the girl who had delivered it.

"Lady Ernestine is asking for Lady Morag and wondering where she is," said the servant.

Willow glanced over her shoulder at Morag. "Please give Lady Ernestine our regrets, but since I am tired from making the journey pregnant, my cousin has insisted in staying in the chamber tonight with me."

"Aye, my lady," said the girl with a curtsey, heading away.

Morag ran to the door and stepped around Willow, sticking her head out into the corridor.

"Did anyone else ask for me?" she called after the servant girl.

"Nay, Lady Morag. Not that I know of," the girl answered.

"Thank ye," said Morag with a frown, closing the door and heading over to the table by the fire where Willow set up the food.

"You can't hide away in here ignoring him forever," said Willow, settling herself on the chair and breaking off a piece of bread. She handed half to Morag.

"I'm no' hungry," said Morag with a shake of her head.

"Good, because I am starved and eating for two." Willow placed both pieces of bread in front of her. "You have really gotten yourself into a mess, Morag."

"I ken." Morag wrapped her arms around her and gazed into the fire.

"What are you going to do?"

"I dinna ken. My da is goin' to kill Bedivere and then he is goin' to kill me."

"Well, you shouldn't have been acting like a strumpet and going to bed with a man before you were married. Humph," she said with a breath of air from her mouth. "And you used to call me a strumpet! At least I waited until after the wedding to consummate it."

"Sorry about that, Willow. I guess I was just so excited to have someone to love that I didna think."

"Since when do you care about love? I have never heard you talk this way before."

Morag felt an aching in her heart. "Since I met Sir Bedivere, I have fallen in love with him verra quickly."

"What are you saying, you silly girl?" Willow poured herself a goblet of wine from the decanter. "You knew Sir Bedivere before, when he wanted to marry me."

"Barely. Besides, that is different. Before, he was interested in ye, no' me."

"Oh, I see. You just like the attention." Willow helped herself to some whitefish, using her finger to scoop it onto her spoon.

"Willow, I have to tell ye somethin' else." Morag decided she would no longer stay quiet. What she needed was a friend to talk to. "When I was at the secret garden, I was bein' mentored by an old woman named Mazelina."

Willow took a bite of food, concentrating on her meal instead of looking at Morag. "What are you talking about? No one has lived in the cottage since Imanie died."

"She said she is Imanie's sister."

Willow swallowed and took another sip of wine. "I never heard Imanie say she had a sister."

"But it's true."

"Really?" Willow looked at her as if she thought it was all a made-up story. "So, tell me, what did she teach you?"

"She taught me . . . she said that . . . I dinna ken exactly. She was mysterious and answered my questions with questions of her own."

"Morag, you always did want attention, and thought you could get it by gossiping or making up things. I have no time or patience for your games."

"But I swear I am tellin' ye the truth!"

Willow wiped her hands on a cloth, rubbed her stomach and waddled over to the bed. "Instead of concocting silly stories, you really need to figure out what you're going to do about Bedivere." Willow yawned and stretched and lay down on the bed. "After all, I don't think my father, Uncle Rowen, or your father are going to want an assassin in the family."

"Willow, dinna tell them about this," begged Morag. "Please."

"Morag, they need to know." Willow turned her head on the pillow and closed her eyes as she continued talking. "I am sure glad I wasn't the one to marry him. How horrible would that have been?"

"Give me a little more time," Morag pleaded with her cousin. "I need to figure out what to do. Please dinna say a word about it to anyone until I have a chance to fix things."

"All right, I will stay quiet for now." Willow pulled the blanket over her and turned on her side. "But I sincerely think you've made a grave mistake, Cousin. There is no way you are going to be able to undo the damage that you've already done."

CHAPTER 16

"Where is Morag?" Bedivere asked Percival in the great hall the next morning. "I haven't seen her since yesterday when we returned to the castle in the rain."

Percival shrugged his shoulders. "I went to her chamber but Lady Willow told me Morag wasn't coming down for the meal."

"Why? What's wrong?" he asked in alarm. "Is she ill?"

"Nay, I don't think so," said Percival, reaching over the high table on the raised dais to grab a sweetmeat from the tray. He popped it into his mouth as he spoke. "She looked fine to me. She was standing by the fire, pacing back and forth."

"I need to talk to her," he whispered. "I cannot wait another minute." Bedivere stood up, not waiting for the next course to be served. It was imperative he speak to Morag and he didn't like the way she'd been ignoring him. She had to already know his secret.

"Sir Bedivere, leaving so soon?" Lord Whitmore leaned over from the other end of the table to see him.

"I have something I need to do," Bedivere made the excuse.

"Well, then, Lord Rook, I guess I'll have to keep you company for a while."

Bedivere stopped in his tracks when he heard Lord Whitmore say this.

"Thank you, Lord Whitmore, I'd like that," replied Rook. "Mayhap, we can get to know each other better." Rook tucked a long strand of black hair behind his ear and reached over for more roasted goose.

Bedivere groaned inwardly and sat back down. There was no way he could leave now. If he did, Rook could be dead before he returned.

* * *

MORAG STARED out the open window, lost in her thoughts, disturbed when there was a knock at the door.

"You really should have a handmaid for things like this," said Willow, waddling across the floor and pulling open the door. "Sir Bedivere," she said.

Morag's heart jumped when she saw Bedivere standing at the door. He looked at her from across the room and the pain in his eyes almost broke Morag's heart.

"I need to talk to Morag."

Morag nodded silently to Willow to let him in. Bedivere stepped inside and glanced down at Willow. "Alone, if you please."

After Morag gave her cousin another nod, Willow

answered. "Of course," she said, glancing nervously back at Morag before heading out the door.

Bedivere stepped inside and closed the door, bolting it behind him. His action scared her, and she now wondered if he had come to kill her. As he made his way toward her, she backed up to the window.

"Dinna touch me or I'll scream," she warned him.

He stopped and scowled at her. "I have been trying to talk to you for days and I only bolted the door because I don't want to be interrupted again."

"Please, dinna kill me."

"Kill you?" His eyebrows dipped and he shook his head. "I see Willow spilled my secret after all. It seems no one in your family can keep their mouth shut."

"If I would have kent ye were a blood-thirsty killer, I never would have let ye near me," she spat, gripping the sill of the window behind her.

"Morag, I admit, I am an assassin, but you need to give me a chance to explain." He took another step toward her.

"Nay!" She held up a halting hand. "Ye led me on and even took my virginity. How could ye do that? Ye fooled me, and I believed ye really loved me."

His expression turned dour and she saw despair wash across his face. "I do love you," he said in a low voice.

"Nay! Ye are just sayin' that because ye want somethin' from me."

"All I want is for you to hear me out."

"I canna believe I let ye –"

Her words were cut off as Bedivere reached out, pulling her into his arms and kissing her so passionately that, for a moment, she forgot about all her troubles or that he could easily kill her.

"That's better," he said, running a hand over her hair and looking deeply into her eyes. "Now that you're quiet, may I tell you about my past?"

Her heart beat rapidly and she didn't know what to do. Her head told her to shout out and call for help, but her heart told her that he would never hurt her. Listening for the answer within her, like Mazelina told her to do, she finally answered. "Go ahead."

He led her to the bed and they sat next to each other. Then he started to explain. "I wasn't always an assassin, and it wasn't by choice."

"What do ye mean?" she asked, taking a deep breath and releasing it slowly.

"When my father was hung for conspiring to kill the king, my family and I were thrown into the dungeon at Whitmore."

"Yer faither wanted to kill my cousin, Richard?" Her body tensed in anticipation. She didn't relax until he rubbed her back gently and continued to explain.

"I don't believe my father was part of any such thing. However, it was my word against Lord Whitmore's."

"Lord Whitmore? The man who came to your chamber with your squire? Or should I say, your brother?"

"Aye. Whitmore is an advisor to the king. And Percival is one of my eight siblings."

"Ye have that many brothers and sisters?"

"I do. And even the twins, at only seven years of age, were imprisoned as well."

"Nay, tell me it isna so." Morag couldn't even imagine such a horrible situation.

"I had to do something to save my family from being killed. That's when Lord Whitmore told me that if I agreed to be the king's assassin, he would make a deal with me. For every man I stopped from trying to kill Richard, one person of my family would be set free."

"That's what those notches in the hilt of yer sword were."

"Aye, I am sad to say, it is true. Those eleven notches were for the eleven men I was ordered to kill. I didn't want to kill anyone, but I had no choice, Morag. Don't you see? If I didn't, I would lose my family and I couldn't allow that to happen."

"Oh, Bedivere, I had no idea." She reached out and took his hands in hers.

"No one did," he said. "The whole incident with my father and my family was kept quiet."

"So is yer family safe now?"

"My aunt, uncle, brothers, and sisters have all been set free. They are living in a small shack on Whitmore's demesne. However, I have one more kill to make before my poor mother is released."

"How long has she been there, Bedivere?"

"It's been two years now."

Morag shuddered at the thought. She'd seen the conditions of the dungeons in several castles and couldn't even imagine staying in a cell for one night.

"If ye are killin' off bad men who want to kill King Richard, then it is a guid thing, right?" She smiled slightly and looked into his dark eyes.

"I suppose it is," he answered. "However, recently, I am starting to have doubts that I should have taken Whitmore's word that these men were guilty. I'll never know for sure if they were, and that is something that will haunt me for the rest of my life."

"Why is Lord Whitmore here?" asked Morag curiously.

"He is here because I refused to make my last kill."

"Ye did?" asked Morag. She was afraid to ask but, in her normal nature, she had to know. "Who does he want ye to kill?"

Bedivere hesitated before answering. "It's not just one man, Morag, but three."

"Three?" Morag raised a brow. "I dinna understand."

"I was ordered to kill three men that I'm sure are not plotting to kill Richard at all."

"Who are they?" she asked, feeling a sour taste in her mouth, somehow knowing she wasn't going to like his answer.

"They are three men you know well," he told her. Looking into her eyes, he spoke lowly. "Morag, I was ordered to kill the Legendary Bastards of the Crown!"

Morag couldn't believe what she'd just heard. Her body stiffened and anger as well as fear pumped through her.

"What?" she asked, hoping this was only some sort of sick jest. There was no way it could be true.

"You heard me. I don't like it either. I'm sorry I had to tell you this, but I didn't want to lie to you anymore."

Morag snatched her hands from his and sprang up off the bed. Bedivere jumped up as well and reached out for her.

"Dinna touch me, ye monster!" she cried, backing up against the bedpost with her hands out in front of her for protection.

"Is that how you really see me, Morag?" The look of intense sadness in his eyes was not that of someone with vengeance in his heart. Instead, it seemed as if her words had cut him to the bone. "I never said I was going to do it. If it'll ease your mind, I'm not planning on harming them at all."

"I dinna believe ye," she spat, even though, in her heart, she felt he was telling the truth. "How can ye be so calloused that it doesna even seem to bother ye to take the lives of those I love?"

"Oh, it bothers me, Morag," he answered gruffly. "More than you'll ever know. Do you understand that by denying this order, I am putting my mother's life at stake? If I don't figure out what to do soon, she'll die in Whitmore's dungeon. He might even decide to come after the rest of my family as well."

"Oh, I didna think of that," she said, feeling her heart soften toward him. "Are ye sure ye are no' goin' to hurt my faither or uncles?" She had to ask again, just to be sure.

"I am going to try to help them, not hurt them," he assured her. "But since I refused to kill them, Whitmore has sent two unidentified assassins to do the job instead."

"Nay!" Morag held on to the bedpost for strength. "Bedivere, we need to tell my faither and uncles about this anon."

"We can't." He paced back and forth, dragging a worried hand through his hair. "If they know about it, they will confront Whitmore and then I'll never flush out the hired killers. I want to take out the assassins first so Whitmore won't order them to go back and kill my mother."

"Isna that dangerous? No' only for my faither and uncles but also for ye?"

"It is. However, I feel it is something I have to do."

"But if my faither and uncles ken about the assassins, they can kill them and ye willna have to."

"Nay." Bedivere stopped pacing and released a frustrated breath. "If Whitmore knows that your uncles and father are aware that his men are here, he'll pull them out rather than to risk their lives. No one wants to go up against the Legendary Bastards of the Crown. I want to do away with the threat of the assassins and then we can all sleep a little easier. Morag, tell me that you're certain your father and uncles would never conspire against the king."

"They wouldna do that! Richard is family."

"So was Edward," he reminded her with a raised brow. "Yet everyone knows your father and uncles fought against him."

"True. At one time, they held vengeance in their hearts against their faither, but that was a long time ago. They have changed. They now support the English crown."

"Even your father? After all, it is no secret he has never accepted the English or paid homage to Edward in any way in the past."

Morag was sure her father wouldn't conspire against Richard. Then again, he did have a temper and that could work against him. Still, she wouldn't tell Bedivere how much Reed despised the English because she didn't want to put doubt in his mind. "Nay, my faither would never do that. Plus, he is no' even in England so that should prove his innocence."

Now Morag regretted sending Branton with a missive calling her father to England to compete for the late earl's holdings. She never should have added his name to the list. He would be walking right into a lion's den and it was all her fault.

"Morag, there is something else I haven't told you."

She felt the lump in her throat, not wanting to hear more.

"What is it?" she asked, not wanting any more secrets between them.

"Whitmore thinks I am still taking out one last man in exchange for the release of my mother."

"Who does he think ye are goin' to kill?" She held her breath, waiting for the answer.

"Reed Douglas. Your father," he answered, not able to look at her when he told her. "Whitmore thinks I am still targeting him while his other assassins go after Rook and Rowen."

"Nay! Ye canna hurt my da," cried Morag. "Dinna do it, Bedivere, please!"

"Shhh," he told her, holding up a hand and looking over to the door. "I understand that." Then his hands balled up into fists and his jaw tightened. "However, I don't know what to do. You need to understand, I have to protect my family as well as free my mother."

"Well, dinna hurt my family in order to do that."

"I don't want to." He hung his head, shaking it slightly. "There has to be another way."

"Do ye think Whitmore is somehow really involved in tryin' to kill the king?"

"I don't think so. He has too much to gain by keeping the king alive."

Morag walked across the room to join him. "How is he findin' out that all these men have bad intentions?"

"There are spies everywhere," he explained. "That part doesn't surprise me. But what does surprise me is how rich Whitmore has become in the past two years."

"What do ye mean?"

"Every time I make a kill, Whitmore ends up claiming the

dead man's holdings. I didn't think much of it at first, but it does seem a little suspicious."

"So, Richard is thankful to him, and that's why he gives him the dead man's castle and land?"

"Exactly."

"He sounds greedy."

"He is. Being advisor to the king, he is constantly whispering in Richard's ear and getting everything he wants and more."

Morag's nerves stilled as she now understood Bedivere's dilemma. She wanted more than anything to help him free his mother. "Do ye think the men ye killed were guilty of plottin' against the king or no'?"

"We'll never know. But I'm sure my father was innocent."

Morag paced back and forth in thought. "Mayhap, because my uncles are close to Richard and often advise him unofficially, that has somethin' to do with Whitmore wantin' them dead."

"Possibly." Bedivere crossed the room and stared out the window in thought. "But why would he order me to kill your father? As you said, he's in Scotland and doesn't want anything to do with the English."

"My faither and uncles would die for each other. They are verra close," explained Morag. "If anyone killed my uncles, Rook and Reed, I am sure my faither would avenge their deaths."

Bedivere turned to her. "You're right. I think that is it. Morag, you are amazing at this."

"I am?" Morag felt the blush rise to her cheeks. It felt good to be told she was good at something in her life, and this was the first time she ever heard it.

"I think my last kill should be the head of the snake," he told her.

"Whitmore?" asked Morag, a small part of her still hoping he didn't mean her father. "But if ye kill the king's advisor, it is only goin' to bring ye and yer family more trouble."

"Aye," Bedivere agreed. "That's why I am going to have to trick Whitmore into admitting his deception. The king needs to know about this."

"Ye'll also need witnesses that will hear him confess, for when he goes to trial."

"Aye. But in the meantime, I need to get back out there and try to stop those assassins. I won't have the deaths of the bastard triplets on my conscience, too. My mind is already tainted enough."

"I'm goin' to help ye," Morag told him.

Bedivere shook his head and let loose with a breath of air. "Nay. What could you do?" he asked her. "I would rather have you locked away safely inside your chamber until I can get things under control. I don't want to have to worry about you because it'll distract me. And if I'm distracted, someone is going to end up dead."

"If someone is out there tryin' to kill my faither and uncles, I assure ye there is nothin' in the world ye can do to keep me behind locked doors. I am goin' to help ye whether ye like it or no.'" Morag crossed her arms over her chest as she took a stand. Her chin rose as she challenged him to tell her otherwise. This decision felt good. It felt right. It was something Morag had to do, no matter how frightened she was deep down. She would push away her fear and her nerves and act like a strong woman for the first time in her life.

Bedivere hesitated and, for a moment, Morag honestly

thought he was going to object. But then with a slight nod of his head, he agreed. "All right. But you have to keep this a secret. Plus, I need you to promise to stop going off into the woods without an escort."

"I promise," answered Morag, knowing there was no reason to return to the secret garden again since Mazelina had left her.

Bedivere walked over and took Morag by the shoulders. Staring deeply into her eyes, she felt that whatever he was about to say was from his heart. "I love you, Morag. And I won't allow harm to come to you. When this is all over and my family, as well as yours is safe, and Whitmore is behind bars, I will marry you just like we planned."

"Really?" Morag was so surprised that he still wanted her that it took her breath away. "Then ye are no' goin' to abandon me like everyone else? And ye want to truly be my husband after all?"

"I promise you, I will never abandon you," he said in a breathy whisper, kissing her atop the head, pulling her against his chest in a protective hug. "I want more than anything to be your husband. Together, we will find a way to save my mother and stop the assassins."

"I will help ye, Bedivere. Just tell me what to do."

He released her and took a step back. "I need you to get out there and listen to all the gossip you can."

"What?" Morag asked, this being the last thing she expected him to say. "Nay, I canna do that. I made a promise never to gossip again."

"But I need you to gossip! In doing so, you will get others to talk as well. And with a little luck, your skill of meddling into everyone's affairs will be an asset. We'll not only be able to find and stop the assassins, but we'll be able to put Whitmore behind bars where he belongs."

"So ye really want me to gossip?" Morag found this plan interesting but confusing.

"Yes. More than anything."

"But I thought gossip was a bad thing," she said, struggling to understand what she was being asked to do.

"Not in this case. In this case, it'll be used for good."

"Use my gossip for a guid purpose," Morag whispered to herself, remembering the words of Mazelina. Perhaps, if she took her vice and turned it into a virtue, she'd be able to accomplish something amazing like her sister and cousins after all. "All right, I'll do it!" she said in excitement, knowing it was going to be dangerous, but also the most important thing she would ever do in her life. "I'll use my skill of gossipin' to find out all we need to ken and we'll make things rights for ye, Bedivere. No one should have to be put through the trials ye've been through lately." She reached up and kissed him gently on the mouth. "Yer past doesna matter to me because I understand now why ye did the things ye had to do. If I were in yer position, I would have done the same to help my family."

"You are going to be helping your family now as well as mine," he told her.

"Aye," she said, not wanting to waste any more time. "I only hope we are no' too late."

CHAPTER 17

*M*orag made her way down to the kitchen the next morning to talk with the servants.

"Lady Morag," said Agnes, the head cook. "What can I get for you?"

"Nothin', Agnes," said Morag, scanning the kitchen and the hustle and bustle of the morning bedlam. "I just decided to see how things were goin' in the kitchen, that's all."

"Coming through, excuse me," said a man carrying a large wooden paddle with uncooked loaves of bread. "Oh my pardons, my lady, I did not see you."

"It's all right. Go ahead." Morag continued to talk with Agnes. "I bet it's a lot of work, cookin' for so many people since Lady Ernestine insists on feedin' all the knights and their squires camped outside the gate.

"Aye, it's terrible. I told my lady that we needed more help. So she invited some of the villagers into the kitchen to cook."

"There are new people in here?"

"Aye, many." The woman ground herbs with a mortar and pestle. "Can you hand me a knife, Lady Morag?"

"Of course," she said, turning around to get a knife from the block of wood. Her eyes caught on something shiny, half-hidden under a cloak thrown over a bench. Curious, she walked over and moved the cloak to find a thin, sharp, double-edged blade. She held it up to inspect it.

"Nay, not that," called Agnes from the other side of the table. "I would never use a knife like that to prepare food. That is more for hunting and gutting carcasses. Bring me the smaller one please."

Before Morag could do as asked, a man rushed over and snatched the knife from her, sticking it into his waist belt. "Don't touch that," he growled.

"That's Lady Morag, have some respect," spat Agnes, peering over the table.

"My many pardons, my lady," said the man with slight bow. "I wasn't aware there was a lady in the kitchen."

"It's an honest mistake," she said, watching as the man hurried to the other side of the room, looking back at her over his shoulder. "Agnes, who was that?" she asked curiously.

"He's one of the fools here helping out. I've never seen him before, so I am guessing he is a servant of one of the visiting knights."

"Is he any good at preparin' food?"

"Nay. He's ruining all our meat with his obnoxious blades. He's butchering the food so badly that I wish he wasn't even here at all. If I didn't need the help so desperately, I'd tell him to leave."

"Butcherin'," she repeated under her breath. Heading across the room to get a better look at the man, she couldn't find him anywhere. "Did ye see a tall man with a short black beard and mustache pass through here?" she asked a boy from the scullery.

"I'm not sure, my lady. That sounds like every man here," said the boy, making a face.

"I suppose it does." Morag looked around at the busy kitchen and decided she needed to try to find the mysterious man on her own. She slipped out the back door of the scullery, seeing someone disappear, turning the corner of the keep. Keeping in the shadows, she stayed close to the castle wall. When she got to the corner she peeked around.

Sure enough, there was the man with the knife, talking in hushed voices with Lord Whitmore. They stood behind the henhouse.

"Do it quickly," said Lord Whitmore. "We cannot waste precious time."

Morag crept closer, but stayed hidden, making her way to the henhouse. She tried hard to hear their conversation over the noise coming from the courtyard.

"I won't let you down," answered the man.

Whitmore pulled a pouch of coins from his waist belt and handed it to the man, scanning his surroundings as he did so. "Another bastard is sure to arrive at any time, so now is your chance. I saw Rook headed for the practice yard."

Morag jerked backward hearing Rook's name, accidentally kicking a feed bucket she hadn't noticed was there. When Whitmore's head snapped up, she pulled back out of sight and hid behind a wagon with tall sides, not even daring to breathe. After a minute she slowly peeked out again. Seeing that the men had left, she turned and ran back to the kitchen. Dodging several kitchen workers, she ended up barreling right into someone's chest.

"Oomph! There you are," said Bedivere, reaching out to steady her. "When Willow told me you'd left the room without her, I had hoped you'd be down here and not on your way to the secret garden."

"Oh, Bedivere, ye need to hurry."

"Hurry? What are you talking about?" She pulled him over to a vacant corner and leaned in close to talk so no one would hear.

"I just saw the –" she looked around and leaned in closer. "The assassin."

"You did? Where?" Bedivere had his sword drawn in a second.

"Put that away." Her hand shot out to cover his. "Ye are goin' to attract attention," she said, using her hand to lower his arm. Then she took hold of his arm and nodded and smiled to the kitchen help as she and Bedivere exited into the corridor.

Once they were in a secluded hallway, Morag continued. "I saw him," she said, feeling her heart about beating out of her chest. "He was a tall man with a small black beard and mustache."

"All right, but that sounds like every man here."

"This one has a long blade that Agnes said isn't proper for the kitchen, but more for huntin'. For guttin' a carcass."

"Where did he go?" Bedivere was on high alert. He looked across the courtyard but Rook was already at the lists.

"He's goin' to kill Uncle Rook."

"Damn. And Rook is scheduled to joust this morning. I see Lady Ernestine heading for the lists as the competition is about to start."

"Go, Bedivere. Save my Uncle Rook. Please."

"I'm on my way," said Bedivere, taking off at a run toward the practice yard.

"Morag, where have you been all morning?"

Morag turned to find Willow approaching with her hand on her huge stomach and her servant who drove the cart at her side.

Morag looked back, worried for Bedivere as well as her uncle, but decided she needed to keep Willow away from the joust if there was going to be trouble.

"Willow. Why dinna we head to the kitchen to get somethin' to eat? I'm sure ye must be starvin'."

"I am hungry, but I wanted to see Father joust in the tilt-yard. You know how much he likes the joust. He'd give up food before he turned down a chance to do it. It will mean much to him that I am there." The servant boy stepped on the back of Willow's gown and she stopped and turned around with a scowl on her face. "Do be more careful," she scolded, pulling the gown out from under the boy's foot.

"So sorry, my lady," apologized the servant.

"I should have brought along my handmaid," complained Willow. "I'll have to find Lady Ernestine and ask her if I can have one of hers assigned to me during my stay. Have you seen her?"

Morag knew Lady Ernestine was at the lists since Bedivere had just told her. But she couldn't let her cousin, especially not in her condition, be anywhere near the field if someone was about to be killed. She could only hope it wasn't going to be Willow's father.

"Let's go see if Lady Ernestine is in the great hall." Morag took her cousin by the arm and directed her toward the keep once again, feeling very nervous for Bedivere as well as for Rook.

* * *

BEDIVERE HURRIED to the practice yard, barely able to find Rook because the area was so crowded. Then he saw Rook with a squire helping him prepare for the joust. Bedivere trusted no one. Hurrying closer, he watched the squire help Rook don his partial plate armor.

"This is too early for a joust, Sir Rook," said Bedivere, moving through the crowd and stopping next to him.

"I know," answered Rook with a chuckle. "I haven't even had food to break the fast yet. Lord Whitmore told me I was scheduled to joist with someone named Sir Raft. I didn't want to miss it."

"Sir Raft?" Bedivere didn't remember hearing this name before. "Who is he? Do you know him?"

"Nay," said Rook holding out his arm so the squire could buckle his arm piece. "I suppose he is someone the earl knew and Lady Ernestine invited. Perhaps from overseas."

"Where is he?" asked Benedict, looking around the stable.

"I saw a man with a lance go behind the building a minute ago," said the squire. "Mayhap it was Sir Raft, although I don't know him either."

"Cancel the joust for now," Bedivere urged Rook. "Let's go get a bite to eat."

"Whatever for?" Rook pulled on his glove. "Everyone knows I love a good joust. I wouldn't miss this for the world. And even though I told Lady Ernestine I am not competing for the earl's holdings, I will never turn down the opportunity to show off my skills."

Bedivere headed to the back of the stable, keeping to the shadows as he looked for the so-called Sir Raft. Then he saw the man. Dressed in a mail shirt open at the arms, but with no plate armor, this couldn't be a real knight. And as Bedivere snuck closer, he could see the man tying a sharp blade to the tip of his lance. To make matters worse, he was talking with Lord Whitmore.

"Don't let anyone see you do it, and get out as fast as you can afterward," instructed Whitmore.

Bedivere had to strain his ears, but he saw and heard Whitmore giving the assassin instructions.

"Don't worry. I'll be out of here before he hits the ground," snarled the man.

"Good. Now go." Whitmore headed away while the man picked up his helm from the ground.

It was deserted behind the stable, too mucky and with too much filth for anyone to want to come here on purpose. There was no one here now but the assassin with his lance and horse. Bedivere knew what he had to do and didn't think twice.

The assassin rested his lance against the building to put on his helm. He was about get on his horse when Bedivere made his presence known.

"You are not going anywhere and I will die before I let you kill Sir Rook." He stepped out of the shadow with his sword in one hand and a long blade in the other.

The man didn't say a word but, instead, reached for his throwing knife and flung it at Bedivere.

Bedivere moved quickly to the side, getting nicked in the

shoulder as the blade stuck into the wall. He looked down to see his torn tunic and blood oozing from his arm.

"Well, if that's the way you want to play it," said Bedivere, lunging at the man with his sword leading the way. Metal clashed against metal and Bedivere kept the man at bay. He was fast with a blade and skilled enough to easily disarm the man. When the assassin reached for two blades at once and rushed forward, Bedivere made his move. He silently shoved his blade under the armhole of the chain mail and right through the assassin's heart. The assassin fell limp to the ground, his helm falling off in the process.

The straight trumpet split the air and the herald announced that Rook and Sir Raft would be jousting, warning them to line up at the list or forfeit. Bedivere had to think fast. If the phony Sir Raft didn't show up, someone would come looking for him.

Pulling the dead man across the ground and depositing him in a ditch filled with manure, he quickly covered the body with hay. He had to keep anyone from coming back to find him or there would be chaos when they found him dead. Bedivere would be arrested and no one would ever know that there was an assassin who almost killed Sir Rook.

There was only one thing to do. Bedivere was going to have to pretend to be Sir Raft. He took hold of the helm, and climbed atop the horse. After putting on the headpiece he directed the horse to the wall, grabbing the lance. He couldn't use it since it wasn't blunted so he knocked the tip hard against the wall, breaking off the assassin's blade. "That's better," he said with a nod, heading to the practice yard.

Lowering his visor, he looked out to see the herald waving a flag from the center of the rail. Then the sound of thundering hoofbeats upon the ground directed his attention to the powerful Sir Rook. The bastard triplet charged down the list with his shield in hand and his lance pointed straight at Bedivere.

"God's eyes," Bedivere ground out, realizing he didn't have a shield or armor of any kind. He was about to be killed by the man he was trying to protect.

"Don't forget your shield, my lord," called out a boy, handing one up to him at the last second.

Grasping the shield tightly in one hand and the lance in the other, he did all he could to hold on to the horse. His steed took off at a run, heading straight for Rook. Bedivere had never been fond of the joust and neither had he been a knight long enough to be any good at it.

It took all his attention just to hold the shield steady and keep the lance from falling. Plus, he had a hard time staying seated in the saddle. As they met, Rook's lance crashed into his shoulder, and Bedivere shouted out in pain being unseated, hitting the ground hard.

The crowd shouted and cheered for Rook.

Rook jumped off his horse and ran over, extending his arm to help him up. "Allow me to help you, Sir Raft," said Rook. "I didn't realize you weren't wearing armor or I never would have hit you."

"Thank you," said Bedivere, leaving his helm in place so Rook wouldn't know it was him.

"You took a nasty blow to the shoulder." Rook noticed the blood. "I'll call for the healer." When Rook turned around to summon his squire to send the message, Bedivere hurried back behind the stable, taking off the helm.

"Sir Raft? Are you back here?" Rook rounded the building

just as Bedivere threw his helm into the back of a cart of manure. "Sir Bedivere," said Rook. "I'm looking for the man I injured in the joust. Have you seen him?"

Bedivere clutched his cloak around him, hiding his bleeding shoulder. "He just left and said he wouldn't be back."

"He did?" Rook squinted and looked in the other direction. "He must move fast, I don't even see him. Well, how about a bite to eat now? I've worked up an appetite."

When Rook turned back, Bedivere was already out of sight and heading back to the keep.

CHAPTER 18

"Hold still," commanded Morag, pulling the thread and closing up Bedivere's wound.

"Ahhh!" He let out a low growl and took another swig of whiskey. "You've never done this before, have you?" he complained.

"Nay, I havena," Morag admitted. "But I am efficient at stitchin' in the ladies solar, so I dinna see how it is any different," answered Morag.

"It's not the same, and my flesh can attest to it. Now hurry up before Rook returns to the solar."

"I still dinna ken why ye dinna let me call the healer."

"Because I can't draw attention to myself," Bedivere explained. "If Whitmore finds his assassin missing and I'm bleeding, he'll know what I did."

"Oh." Morag tied a knot, leaned over and broke the thread with her teeth. She didn't want to know the answer to her next question but, still, she had to ask. "So how did ye . . . do it," she said with a gulp. Envisioning Bedivere slitting a man's throat wasn't the vision in her head she wanted about the man she was about to marry.

"It's better if you don't know."

"What did ye do with the body?"

"It's in a ditch, but I need to go back and bury it before the birds start pecking at his flesh, alerting someone he's there."

"Ye canna go back there and do that! Ye can barely lift yer arm." Morag put the needle and thread back into the basket and closed the lid. "I'll take care of the task for ye."

"Nay. I would never let you do such a thing and I don't want to hear you say something so foolish again."

"I mean it. I told ye I want to help and I'll do whatever it takes." She didn't honestly want to bury a dead body let alone see or touch it, but she was trying to be supportive. Thankfully, he objected.

The door to the room burst open and Percival entered, followed by a large man, a mature woman, and a whole procession of people, most of them children.

"Percival, what the hell are you doing?" asked Bedivere with a grunt.

"Bedivere," cried one of the young women, running to him and throwing her arms around him. He cried out when she touched his wound.

"Careful, Sister, I am wounded," he explained.

"Sister? So this is yer family?" asked Morag, smiling, taking in the sight of so many siblings.

"I'm Elizabeth. Who are you?" asked the eldest of the girls, standing in front of her brother with her arms spread out protectively.

"I'm Lady Morag Douglas. Nice to meet ye."

Then the big, older man stepped forward, squinting as if

he couldn't see her well. "I am Bedivere's uncle, Theobald. And this is my wife, Joan." He nodded to the woman hanging on to his arm. They both bowed to her and the children followed suit.

"There's no need to bow," said Morag with a smile. She never felt so important in all her life.

Bedivere introduced the rest of his family. "Morag, these are my sisters, Elizabeth, Avelina, Sarah, Claire, and Rhoslyn."

"Don't forget about us," said one of the young boys pushing the girls to the side and coming forward. The second one who looked like the first one's twin, followed.

"And these are my outspoken little brothers, Luther and Averey," added Bedivere, ruffling the hair of one of them. The boy pushed Bedivere's hand away and made a face. "Percival, why did you bring them here?" asked Bedivere. "I thought I told you to keep them put for now."

"I didn't do it. They came on their own," said Percival. "I found them on the road outside the castle."

"We wanted to be by you," said the girl he'd introduced as Sarah.

"We missed you," added Elizabeth.

"And we also miss Mother," said one of the twin boys, Morag wasn't sure which.

"I know," said Bedivere, his eyes flashing over to Morag.

"Oh, who have we here?" Willow appeared in the doorway and entered the room with her father right behind her.

"Bedivere, there you are," said Rook. "I was looking every-where for you. My brother, Rowen, just arrived and I thought the three of us could have an ale together." Rook's eyes lowered to Bedivere's shoulder. "Hurt yourself?" he asked.

"It's nothing," said Bedivere, closing his cloak over his

wound. "Aye, I would like to join you, but I have an errand to attend to first."

"Nothing can be that important that it can't wait," came a voice from the doorway. Rowen, the blond triplet, stood there with his daughter, Maira, at his side.

"Maira!" exclaimed Morag, happy to see her cousin again. "Did Jacob come with ye?"

"He's down in the great hall. He said he wanted to sample the heather ale," answered Maira with a smile.

"Come on, Morag," said Willow. "We'll share some girl talk below stairs. Now, all we need is Fia and it'll be like old times."

"I sent Branton to Scotland to get my faither and I dinna think Fia is comin'," Morag told them.

"Morag, would you mind taking my family to the great hall with you for some food while they're waiting for me?" asked Bedivere.

"I'd be happy to," Morag answered, knowing he needed to get back to bury the body.

"I've never seen such a big castle." Aunt Joan's eyes lit up as she perused the room. "The man who gets the late earl's estate is going to be very lucky."

"Let's go, I'm starving." Percival zigzagged through the crowd, being the first to the door.

"Not you, Brother," Bedivere stopped him. "I'd like you and Uncle Theobald to stay for a moment."

"Whatever for?" whined Percival.

"I have a little errand I need you to help me with that needs immediate attention."

CHAPTER 19

*B*edivere did his best to avoid Lord Whitmore, heading out to the stables the next morning. He had come here looking for the last assassin, planning on asking the stable boy questions to see if anyone seemed out of place.

Thankfully, Lady Ernestine loved the fact that Bedivere's family was there and was treating them like royalty, letting them stay at the castle. She was so thankful that Bedivere had saved her from the burning building that she gave his family extra care and attention. That was a good thing because with all the attention they were getting, it protected them from men like Whitmore. And with Willow and Maira spending so much time with Morag, he felt she was protected as well. He'd heard stories that Maira was a force to be reckoned with and could use a blade just as well as most men.

He would take a quick look around and then head back to the great hall and stick close to Rowen. The assassin was most likely waiting for the opportune moment to make his move.

"I figured you'd show up here sooner or later," came a voice from behind him.

Bedivere stopped in his tracks and groaned inwardly, seeing Lord Whitmore leaning against a stall.

"Whitmore," mumbled Bedivere. "What do you want?"

"Leave us," Whitmore instructed the stable boy.

"Aye, my lord." The boy bowed quickly and ran out to the courtyard.

"My man has gone missing," said Whitmore. "Would you happen to know where I could find him?" Whitmore stood up straight, his dark eyes drilling into Bedivere.

"What man?" he asked, watching Whitmore's face screw up.

"You know damned well who I mean. Now, tell me what you did with him."

"All I know is that he lost the joust yesterday to Rook and then disappeared. He was probably so embarrassed that he failed that he hightailed it out of here."

"Stop it, you fool!" Whitmore grabbed Bedivere by the front of the tunic. "I know you had something to do with his disappearance, and I promise you that you'll pay for it."

When he yanked on Bedivere's clothes, Bedivere grimaced slightly at the pulling against his stitches. Whitmore noticed and yanked his tunic aside.

"You seem to be hurt in the exact spot I heard Sir Raft was wounded. I find that too much of a coincidence."

"Let go of me." Bedivere pushed the man's hands away. "You need to leave here because our work together is finished."

"It's not finished until I say so. Since my man failed to do his job, it looks like the next one will have double the work now."

"Why are you doing this?" snarled Bedivere.

"I am eliminating three threats against the king."

"We both know that the bastard triplets have no plan to hurt or kill the king. So tell me, what is the real reason you want them gone?"

Whitmore looked down his nose and he donned his gloves. "Do your job and don't ask questions."

"I told you, I'm done doing your dirty work," said Bedivere.

"You have one more job to do or you can say goodbye to your mother forever."

Bedivere stopped pushing the man with his words. He had to watch his step until he was able to free his mother. "Reed Douglas isn't even here. I can't do the job if I don't have a target."

"Then finish off Rook instead, I don't care. But you owe me and I won't forget it."

"Bedivere, are ye in here?" Morag showed up at the door to the stable and stopped in her tracks when she saw him talking to Whitmore. "Oh, I didna ken ye were busy."

"He's not busy now, but will be soon." Whitmore turned and pushed past Morag, exiting the stable.

"What is it, Morag?" asked Bedivere, feeling as if the walls were closing in around him. "What do you want?"

"I was comin' to tell ye that Uncle Rowen said he's no' feelin' well today and that he's goin' to call the healer for a potion. It seems he drank too much ale last night."

"Have you found out anything else by talking to the servants?"

"It's been hard now that my cousins and yer family are here, but there is a bit of gossip goin' around the kitchen that I think might interest ye."

"What is it?"

"I overheard one of the scullery maids tellin' a page that she heard the guards talkin' after she bedded one of them last night."

"Why should this concern me? I don't care what they do behind closed doors."

"She said one of the beggars was wearin' a ring that he said he found on a slain man in the woods."

"Dead man?" Bedivere's ears perked up. "Who was it?"

"I dinna ken. I asked the page afterwards and he said that the guards didna want to upset Lady Ernestine so they buried the body in the woods for now. There are so many people here for the choosin' of the earl's successor in two days' time, that they didna want to cause a ruckus by lettin' everyone know a man has been murdered."

"Murdered? Which guards know about this?"

"I'm no' sure. Did ye want me to find the girl and ask her?"

"Nay." Bedivere turned and quickly saddled his horse. "There's no time. Do you know where they buried the man?"

"The scullery maid said the body was buried in a shallow grave behind the biggest rowan tree at the entrance to the forest."

"Thank you, Morag. This is good information. But I need to know who was murdered because it could tell us a lot about what is going to happen next." He climbed atop the horse.

"Wait! Where are ye goin'?"

"I'm going to find the body to see if I can get more information."

"Then I'm comin' with ye."

Before Bedivere could object, Morag was climbing up atop the horse as well.

"Well, all right," he said, knowing she might be helpful since he didn't know people at the castle. "But we've got to hurry before something horrible happens."

"Was it somethin' Whitmore said that has ye so worried?"

"It's what he didn't say that concerns me the most. Hold on, because we're riding fast and stopping for nothing."

They took off over the drawbridge and through the crowd of knights and villagers gathered just outside the castle. It didn't take long to get to the tree that Morag pointed out to him.

"That's it. That's the tree," said Morag. Bedivere brought the horse to a stop. He dismounted and helped her down as well.

"Fresh dirt," he said, pointing to a plot of earth that had recently been dug.

"Do ye think that is where the body is buried?" Morag made a face.

"I'm pretty sure. But there is only one way to find out." Bedivere grabbed a thick branch and used it to dig in the earth. It didn't take long before he found the body, flipping it over to see that the man's throat had been slit. "It's the work of an assassin," he told Morag.

"Are ye sure?" Morag kept her distance and looked the other way, not wanting to lay eyes on the dead man.

"I'm sure." Bedivere had slit enough throats in his life to recognize the work of an assassin.

"I canna look," said Morag, holding her hand over her nose and mouth trying not to inhale the putrid smell.

"I don't recognize the man and need you to tell me if you know him, Morag. Take a look."

"I canna," she answered, looking the other way. "Dinna ask me to do that."

"Morag, your uncles' lives depend on this, and mayhap my mother's life as well. You said you'd help me. Now, come here and tell me if you've ever seen this man before."

"All right," she finally agreed, biting her lip and stretching her neck to see the man's face. Her eyes opened wide and she gasped. And then she turned on her heel and held her arms around her in the protective hold she always used.

"Do you recognize him?"

"I do," she said, her voice trembling and her bottom lip quivering. "It's Maurice, the castle's healer," she said, wiping a tear from her eye.

"The healer," said Bedivere, standing up, suddenly stiffening when he remembered something Morag had said. "Didn't you tell me Rowen wasn't feeling well and went to the healer for a potion? How could he when the healer is here?"

"Och, Bedivere, I forgot all about it."

"What did you forget?"

"The other night when Lady Ernestine was hurt in the fire, I called to a man that I thought was the castle healer, but he wasna."

"I vaguely remember. What do you mean?" Bedivere wiped off his hands and headed toward her.

"I mean, he was wearin' a cloak that looked like the healer's and had a bag of balms and ointments too. But I had never seen him before. And then he disappeared into the crowd. Oh nay, ye dinna think –"

"Quickly, get on the horse, Morag. We need to get back to the castle at once because I think your Uncle Rowen is in grave danger."

CHAPTER 20

As soon as they got to the gate and through the crowd, Morag saw her father as well as her mother, brothers, and Fia with her baby. They were in the courtyard talking with Willow, Rook, and Maira, and it was obvious they had just arrived.

"Oh no! It's my da," Morag said, holding on to Bedivere from behind. As soon as he stopped the horse they both dismounted.

Reed looked up and his face clouded over when he saw Morag riding with Bedivere.

"Morag, come here," Reed ground out, motioning her over with a wave of his arm.

"Go on," said Bedivere. "I'll get to the solar and stop anything bad from happening to your Uncle Rowen. Hopefully, I'm not too late."

"Bedivere, dinna leave me alone with my faither," whispered Morag. "I ken that look on his face and the angry tone of his voice. Someone must have told him that we are betrothed and he doesna like it."

"If I stay here, Rowen will die."

"Then I'll come with ye." She gripped his arm tightly for support.

"Be strong, Morag. I'll be back to talk to your father, but first I've got a job to do. If you slow me down, I might not get there in time."

"Then go," she told him, releasing his arm and slowly raising her chin. "I will do this on my own."

As soon as Bedivere ran off toward the keep, Reed stormed up, looking madder than hell.

"Da, I am so glad ye decided to come to Rothbury after all." Morag reached up and kissed her father on the cheek. "I think ye might win the earl's holdin's."

"I am no' here for castles and lands. I only came because I am worried about ye and so is yer mathair."

"Now, Reed, I heard that," said Morag's mother, Maggie, walking up with Fia, holding her baby. "That's no' true. Ye were the only one worried about our daughter."

"Fia, ye came and brought the bairn." Morag hugged her sister and gave the baby a kiss on the cheek.

"I wasna goin' to miss yer weddin'," said Fia.

"Oh. Ye heard."

"Of course we heard," spat Reed. "Branton told us ye were kissin' Sir Bedivere."

"Branton," she said under her breath, looking at him talking with her cousins and brothers across the courtyard. He looked up, smiled, and waved.

"I kent ye were goin' to end up marryin' him," said Fia. "And when we got here and Willow told us ye were betrothed, I realized I was right."

"Willow told ye?" She glared at Willow across the courtyard next. Willow raised her chin and looked the other way, pretending not to see her. "Faither, it is true I am goin' to marry Bedivere. He is a verra nice man and will take care of me and protect me, so ye dinna have to worry."

"Protect ye?" Reed's face turned red and his hands balled up into fists. He leaned over and his face came close when he spoke. "I hear the man is an assassin. He'll kill ye is what he'll do."

"Dinna believe gossip, Da."

"Is it true?" asked her mother. "Willow told us his secret."

"Willow is naught but a gossip," answered Morag, shooting her cousin a dirty glance.

"Morag, what kind of trouble are ye courtin'?" asked Fia, bouncing her baby on her hip. "Ye had better be careful. Ye dinna want to marry a man like that."

"Me? Fia, ye married the man who kidnapped ye. I dinna think ye should be judgin' me."

"I'm goin' to kill Bedivere before he touches ye." Reed squinted his eyes and pursed his mouth. "He hasna touched ye, Morag, has he?"

Morag's stomach clenched and she felt as if she were going to retch. She wrapped her arms around her and looked to the ground. What had she been thinking, sending Branton with a missive to bring her father here? And why had she let Bedivere talk her into signing up her father and uncles when all it did was put their lives in danger? She wanted to tell her father everything, but it wasn't her place to do so. She needed Bedivere by her side. Plus, she didn't want to do anything to jeopardize the life of his poor mother.

"Look. Everyone is goin' into the great hall now for the

meal," interrupted Fia. "Da, Uncle Rook is callin' ye over. We'd better hurry if we want to get a seat."

The crowd piled into the courtyard and headed toward the great hall. Lady Ernestine had invited all the men competing for her husband's holdings and their squires and families who were present, to join in a celebration feast. The castle was large and elaborate since the late earl had a lot of money. There was no shortage of food, wine, or ale. The lady of the castle wanted to make her last gathering one to remember.

"Reed, get your arse over here. I'm hungry," shouted Rook to his brother.

"Let's go, Reed." Maggie took her husband's arm. "We can talk about all this later in private. There will be plenty of time."

"This is far from over, Daughter," said Reed, throwing her a menacing glance and heading away with Maggie to the great hall.

As soon as they left, Morag took her sister's arm. "Thank ye for helpin' me ward off the wrath of Da, Fia."

"Morag, ye already slept with Bedivere, didna ye?" asked her sister in concern.

"How did ye ken?"

"I could tell by yer body language." Fia shifted her baby to the other side. "And I can also tell that somethin' more than just marryin' Bedivere is troublin' ye. Did ye want to tell me what it is?"

Morag bit her lip, wanting more than anything to tell her sister about Bedivere's troubles as well as to tell her about Mazelina and every thought that had been going through her head since she got here. But she was sworn to secrecy. To keep quiet was the hardest thing she had ever had to do in her life. Besides, she had already broken her silence when she had told Willow, so she didn't want to tempt fate any more than that.

"I wish I could, Fia, but I canna break a promise I made no' to gossip."

"If ye're involved, it's no' gossip," Fia pointed out.

"But if I say anythin' right now . . . somethin' bad might happen."

"Then all the more reason to say somethin'. If ye willna tell me, then at least tell Da. Mayhap, he can help ye."

"Nay, Fia, no' Da! He's the last person I can tell my secret to right now."

* * *

BEDIVERE SLOWLY PUSHED OPEN the solar door, holding his dagger under his cloak. The assassin dressed like the healer finished pouring a potion from a bottle into the cup that Rowen held in front of him. It was poison. Bedivere was sure of it. He had to stop Rook before he drank it.

"Sir Rowen, how are you feeling?" Bedivere held his dagger under the folds of his robe as he approached the table.

Rowen was about to take a drink and stopped, putting the goblet on the table and looking up to answer.

The assassin's head jerked around and he silently glared at Bedivere.

"I'm about to find out," said Rowen. "The healer has made a potion that he says is guaranteed to stop my stomach from aching."

"I'm sure he has." Bedivere strolled closer to the table, keeping his eye on the assassin at all times. "I came to tell you that Reed and his family have just arrived.

"Reed is here? I'd like to see him," said Rowen.

"The crowd is filling up the great hall and Reed said if you don't come right away, he'll give away your spot at the table."

"That sounds like my two-faced brother," Rowen answered with a chuckle. "He'll probably do it anyway just so there's more food for him. I'd better get down there right away."

He stepped away from the table but the healer stopped him. "Sir Rowen, you had better drink your healing potion before you even think of eating a thing."

"Aye, I almost forgot." Rowen reached out for it, but Bedivere couldn't let him drink the poison. He reached out for the cup at the same time.

"I'll get it for you," Bedivere told him, purposely knocking over the cup. The potion spilled out and spread across the table, dribbling down to the floor.

"You bastard, you did that on purpose," growled the healer under his breath.

"What did you call him?" asked Rowen, looking at the healer in a not-so-friendly manner, not liking the word bastard used in his presence.

"Lord Rowen, I'll make you another potion, don't leave," said the man.

"Nay, I don't think I need it any longer." Rowen glared at him. "You don't seem very respectful for a healer. I'm surprised Lady Ernestine keeps you around."

"My apologies, my lord," said the man, bowing and putting on a grand show.

"Come, Sir Bedivere, let's go to the great hall to meet my brother," said Rowen.

"I'll meet you there," Bedivere told him. "Since I'm responsible for the spill, it is only fair that I stay and clean up the mess."

"Have it your way." Rowen shook his head and headed out the door, closing it behind him.

As soon as the door closed, the assassin pulled a dagger out of his medicine bag and lunged at Bedivere. Bedivere jumped back, stumbling a little but righted himself again.

"Why did you have to interfere?" snarled the man, gritting his teeth. "I almost had him where I wanted him."

"You will kill him over my dead body," Bedivere told him.

"I will gladly kill you first, and then all three of the bastards as well."

They struggled with each other, fighting and holding each other's hands back from being stabbed. Bedivere was thrown against the wall next to the window. The man was very strong. And when he ran at him again with his blade in his outstretched arm, Bedivere quickly rolled to the side, reaching out and pushing the man right out the open window.

The assassin screamed as he fell to the ground several stories below. Bedivere ran to the window and looked out. It was the back of the castle and the man fell right on a rake that was left there to clean out the gong pit.

The door opened and Percival hurried in. "Brother, Morag told me you were up here and I came right away to see if I could help." He looked around the room. "Where is everyone?"

"Lord Rowen is down at the great hall where I'd like to be

right now," Bedivere told him. He pushed his dagger into his waist belt and brushed off his clothes.

"All right. Let's go eat," said Percival with a smile, liking the idea.

"In a moment," said Bedivere. "We've got one task to attend to first."

$\mathcal{T}$he meal was nearly over before Morag spotted Bedivere and his brother walking into the great hall.

"Bedivere, up here." Morag sat at the dais between her father and Lady Ernestine, waving her hand wildly in the air.

"Dinna call that murderer over here," Reed mumbled under his breath.

"Da," Morag whispered. "Dinna call him that."

"Well, that's what he is. And ye will no' go anywhere near the man, do ye hear me?"

"Lady Morag, I have all the plans made for your wedding on the morrow," said Lady Ernestine, smiling widely. "You and Sir Bedivere will be married in the morning and I've already decided on who I'd like to nominate to claim my late husband's holdings. I'm sure King Richard will agree."

"My daughter will no' be marryin' anyone," spat Reed.

"I'm sorry." Lady Ernestine glanced at Morag. "Morag, I thought you'd talked to your father and already had his permission."

"No' yet," she said, making a face. "But I'm sure my da will agree to the marriage once he gets to ken my betrothed a little better. Mayhap, I need just a little more time."

"Ye dinna need more time and ye dinna need to bother because ye'll never convince me," Reed told her. "Morag, ye will no' be marryin' that sad excuse for a man, and neither are we stayin' any longer in Rothbury. We will leave for Scotland first thing in the mornin'." He pushed away from the table in a huff.

"Sir Bedivere saved my life," Lady Ernestine told Reed. "I assure you, he is a good man."

"Harumph!" scoffed Reed. "If he saved yer life, I am sure it was by accident, because men like Bedivere only ken one thing and I assure ye it has nothin' to do with preservin' a life." He stormed away from the table.

"What did that mean?" Lady Ernestine picked up her goblet to drink.

"It doesna matter." Morag got up and hurried over to her mother. "Mathair, talk some sense into Da. Please. Canna ye convince him to let me marry Sir Bedivere?"

"I'll try," said Morag's mother, reaching out and putting her hand over Morag's. "But ye ken yer faither is a verra stubborn man."

"He is ruinin' my life! He doesna care about me at all."

"Nay, Morag, that's no' true." Maggie's brows dipped in concern. "Yer faither loves ye verra much and is only tryin' to protect ye."

"I'm no' the one that needs protectin'. He is!" Morag hurried away to join Bedivere.

"Morag, I'm sorry I'm late." Bedivere looked over to Reed

who was plowing his way across the crowded room, heading out the door. "What's got your father so upset?"

"Our marriage," she told him. "He hasna agreed to it. Yet. But I'll convince him of it in time. How did things go with the . . . healer?" Morag's eyes darted back and forth.

"It's all taken care of. Now, we only need to worry about Whitmore. Have you seen him anywhere?" Bedivere made a quick scan of the room.

"Nay, and neither do I want to. I dinna want anythin' to do with the man ever again."

"Morag," called out Fia. "We've decided to go for a stroll around the castle grounds." Morag looked up to see her sister, along with Willow and Maira, headed right for her. "I saw how upset Da was and thought ye might like to talk with us."

"Well, I'm no' sure." Morag's eyes flew over to Bedivere. She'd yet to find out what their next move was, plus she wanted to talk to him more about how to convince her father that Bedivere was a good man. Without revealing his secrets, it was going to be nearly impossible to change her father's mind.

"Go on," instructed Bedivere. "It would be good for you to forget about your troubles for a while and spend some time with your sister and cousins."

"If ye're sure," said Morag, still hesitant to leave him.

"I have some more business to attend to anyway, so I'll see you later." Bedivere leaned over and gave Morag a quick kiss on the mouth before heading away.

"He's actually not a bad looking man," observed her cousin, Maira.

"Too bad he's an assassin," said Willow under her breath. "Morag, you want nothing to do with that man."

"He's a guid man," Morag assured the girls. "If I could tell ye the secret I promised to keep to myself, ye would understand this, too."

"You want us to believe you're harboring a secret?" asked Willow with a chuckle.

"We know you all too well," added Maira. "If there was a secret, you would have told us by now."

"There is one. Ye have to believe me," she tried to convince them.

"Morag, I have Mathair watchin' the baby for now," said Fia. "Why dinna we go for a walk to help clear yer head?"

"My head is clear," she protested. However, by the looks they gave her, she realized she was going to have to tell them something more before they'd ever believe her. "I've also been gettin' mentored by Imanie's sister, Mazelina."

"Morag, Imanie doesna have a sister," Fia told her.

"How do ye ken?"

"If she does, she never mentioned it to us," said Maira.

"This is another one of Morag's made up stories," said Willow with sigh.

"Nay, it's true," she tried to convince them.

"Then show her to us," challenged Willow, rubbing her huge stomach. "That is, unless she is naught but made up in your mind."

"Stop it. All of ye," cried Morag. "It is true and I will prove it." She looked across the great hall to see Bedivere talking with Whitmore. Bedivere had warned her not to go out unescorted into the woods. But she wouldn't be unescorted if her sister and cousins were with her. Maira would protect her since she was skilled with a sword. Mayhap, she'd even let Branton come along. The assassins were dead now and Whitmore was here, so what would it matter? She had to convince the girls that she wasn't lying.

"How are you going to prove it?" asked Maira.

"I'll let ye meet Mazelina," Morag told them.

"Where is she?" asked Fia.

"I am no' sure. But she was in the secret garden so let's take a ride and see if she is still there."

"The secret garden?" asked Fia. "I dinna think I should go. I promised Alastair I wouldna have anythin' to do with the Followers of the Secret Heart anymore."

"Alastair isna here, Sister," Morag pointed out. "And ye are no' bein' involved in anythin'. We are goin' for a harmless ride to a deserted garden, and that's all."

"Well, I suppose it'll be all right then," agreed Fia.

"I'm glad I didn't make my husband any kind of foolish promise like that," said Willow. "I'm ready to go meet Mazelina."

"I'll be sure to bring my sword to protect us," offered Maira.

"Let's bring Branton along as well," Morag suggested.

"Branton?" asked Maira. "Whatever for?"

"I promised Bedivere I wouldna leave the castle without an escort," Morag explained.

"Then Branton it is," said Fia. "Now, let's take one last ride to the secret garden for old time's sake."

* * *

BEDIVERE NOTICED Morag leaving the great hall with her sister and cousins and was glad she was surrounded by those she loved. Hopefully, in a matter of time, he'd free his mother and he, too, could be with his entire family again.

"You look as if you're up to no good," Whitmore told Bedivere. "What did you do? And why is Sir Rowen here in the great hall? I thought my man took him above stairs for a little meeting."

"That meeting was cut short for your man, sorry to say." Bedivere flashed a smile.

"You don't know what you're doing," Whitmore ground out. "You'll pay for this, you fool."

"Nay, I won't." Bedivere directed the man to a corner where they could speak in private. "Neither will I finish my last job."

"You have to. If you don't, you'll never see your mother again."

Bedivere was caught in the middle of a hard situation and needed to remedy the matter once and for all.

"I am willing to make some kind of deal for the release of my mother and to be set free of anything to do with you ever again," he told the man.

Whitmore thought for a second and then nodded. "All right. We'll make a deal."

"Sir Bedivere," someone called out. "I'd like to have a word with ye please."

Bedivere looked up to see Reed waving him down from across the hall. It was the last thing he needed right now.

"Meet with me in the orchard tonight and we'll discuss this," said Bedivere, hoping to set up a meeting where Whitmore would confess everything and the bastard triplets were present as witnesses to hear it. If so, he should be able to lock the man away forever and save his mother as well as the bastards.

"Nay, not there. We'll meet somewhere more private. In the woods," said Whitmore. "Meet me at the edge of the earl's lands in an hour."

"Done," said Bedivere. "But don't try to pull anything over on me, or I swear I'll kill you."

"The same goes for me. You had better come alone if you know what's good for you. If not, you'll be sorry."

"Bedivere," ground out Reed, walking up to join them. "I'll have a word with ye regardin' my daughter, Morag."

"Pardon me, but I'll be on my way," said Whitmore.

"Wait!" said Reed, looking at him from the corner of his eye. "Who are ye?"

"This is Lord John Whitmore," said Bedivere, introducing him.

"Whitmore? The advisor to King Richard?" asked Reed.

"I am," said Whitmore with a nod.

"Ye are the man who is convincin' Richard to give ye all the lands and riches of knights and barons that are killed," he spat. "I've heard of ye. My brathairs told me all about ye."

"I d-don't know what you're talking about," stuttered the man.

"Well, dinna think ye'll get Earl Rothbury's fief as well. I'll see to it that Lady Ernestine doesna give it to the likes of ye."

"I think you've got the wrong impression of me," said Whitmore. "I am only here visiting and not competing for the earl's holdings. Now, if you'll excuse me, I need to go."

"I dinna like him," snarled Reed as Whitmore walked away. "My brathairs have told me all about him and we are goin' to do somethin' about it."

"What do you mean?" asked Bedivere.

"He's a crook and needs to be stopped. Even though Richard has never been fond of my brathairs and me because we are his grandfaither's bastard sons, we dinna want to see him fail. We are goin' to talk to him soon and expose Whitmore for who he really is."

That was it, thought Bedivere. Whitmore knew the bastard triplets planned on exposing him to the king and that was why Whitmore wanted Bedivere to kill them. It all made sense now. Bedivere's father probably knew about Whitmore's doings as well and might have been going to expose him to Richard and that's why he was killed.

"I don't like the man either," said Bedivere, "so I'm glad to hear you feel the same way."

"I might no' like Whitmore but I dinna care for ye, either," said Reed. "And once again, Bedivere, ye willna marry my daughter."

"I need to speak with you, as well as Rowen and Rook in private," Bedivere told him.

"About what?"

"It's a matter that I think you will be very interested in. I'd like to take you for a ride into the woods in an hour because there is something I need you to hear."

CHAPTER 22

"Mazelina, are ye here?" Morag called out for the third time, leading the way into the secret garden, followed by the girls as well as Branton.

"I don't see anyone," said Maira, holding her sword at the ready should they need it.

"It's so dead and overgrown that it gives me shivers." Willow pulled her cloak around her, having dismounted her horse.

"It's spring and the new buds will be pokin' their heads out soon," Morag told her.

"I'll watch over the horses and also the gate," offered Branton, taking the reins of the horses from the girls. "I know I'm not supposed to be in the secret garden, so just pretend I'm not here."

"Branton, how can we pretend someone is no' here that we see standin' right in front of us?" asked Morag.

"Probably the same way we're supposed to pretend someone is here when there really isn't anyone," said Willow.

"Mazelina was here," exclaimed Morag. "I didna make her

up. She was trainin' me just like ye all were mentored by Imanie."

"What did she teach you?" asked Maira.

"To use my gossipin' for guid," Morag explained, feeling very foolish since this sounded so addlepated at the moment. "Ye believe me, Fia, right?"

Fia exchanged glances with her cousins. "Perhaps she's in the cottage. Shall we have a look?"

"Yes. I'm sure that is where she is." Morag led the way to the cottage, up the stairs and inside the small enclosure.

"This doesna look as if anyone has lived in here since Imanie passed away," said Fia.

"It's so dusty and dirty," complained Willow.

"Mazelina? Are ye here?" Morag was losing hope that the woman would appear. After all, hadn't she told Morag that she didn't need her anymore and that she could no longer mentor her?

"Where are her things?" asked Maira.

Willow walked over and opened the cupboard. "There's not even a single dirty dish on the table or a scrap of food in the cupboard."

"I dinna understand," said Morag, sinking down into a chair. "She was right here with me. I swear she was."

"There have been no fires here lately." Maira kicked at the old logs in the hearth.

"Morag, is this just another one of your cries for attention?" asked Willow. "I rode through the woods on the back of a horse while six months pregnant, and for what? It's as plain as day that no one has been here so stop your lying."

"I'm no' lyin'!" exclaimed Morag. "I buried my heart brooch atop Imanie's grave wishin' she were alive, and then

Mazelina appeared. She mentored me in secret, so I could feel like a true member of the group."

"If you want to be a member so badly then why did you bury your brooch?" asked Maira.

"I – I suppose it was because I was confused. Here, I'll show ye the brooch in the ground."

They all followed her out to Imanie's grave, taking a moment to say a quick prayer for the old woman's soul.

"It's right here," said Morag, kneeling down and brushing away the dead leaves, digging with her bare hands in the dirt where she'd buried the pin. However, she couldn't find it. "It's no' here," she said in confusion.

The wind picked up causing a shiver to run through her.

"I'm tired and cold," said Willow. "Let's get back to the castle."

"My baby is hungry," said Maira, putting her hand on her pregnant stomach. "And I could go for a bite to eat as well." She shoved her sword into the sheath on her back.

"Ye just ate!" cried Morag. "Give me another minute. I'm sure I'll find the brooch."

Maira and Willow kept walking to their horses.

"Fia, ye've got to believe me," said Morag. "I am no' makin' this up."

"There is no one but us here," Fia answered with a sad shake of her head. "I want to believe ye, ye ken I do. But I think our cousins are right. The wind is pickin' up and we should be gettin' back to the castle."

"Nay! I'm no' goin' until I find Mazelina or the brooch. I am goin' to prove to ye all that I am no' a liar."

The girls mounted their horses and headed to the gate.

"Come on, Morag and Fia. It's getting really windy," Branton called out.

"Go without me. I'm stayin' here to think," answered Morag stubbornly.

"Morag, come with us," pleaded Fia. "Da is no' goin' to like it if we leave ye here alone."

"Then dinna tell him." Morag folded her arms over her chest. "I am no' goin' anywhere and none of ye can make me."

Fia walked over and spoke with the girls and Branton. After a minute, Branton looked over to Morag. "I'll stay with you, Morag."

"I dinna want ye here, Branton." Morag felt tears welling up in her eyes and blinked them away. "I want to be alone."

"Come on, Morag," said Fia. "Dinna act this way."

"Fia, I am no' goin' until I find out what happened to the brooch as well as Mazelina."

Branton talked to the girls once more and then shouted out to Morag. "I'm going to escort the girls back to the castle and I will be back for you right afterwards, Morag. Will you be all right until then?"

"Of course, I will," she said, no longer even caring. "I am safe in the secret garden. This is where I belong. Besides, I'm sure Mazelina will be returnin' at any minute."

She didn't miss the roll of Willow's eyes or the scowl of disbelief on Maira's face. Even her own sister didn't seem as if she believed her.

They left the garden and Morag dug through the dirt once more, not finding the brooch anywhere. Could Mazelina have taken it? But why would she? And was Mazelina real or only a figment of her imagination? She was beginning to wonder if she were going mad. The more she thought about it, the more she realized she had never seen Mazelina eat or even sit down. She wouldn't allow Morag to hug her either. Neither had Morag ever seen the bed covers rumpled or a dish with food left anywhere.

"I am goin' mad," said Morag, wiping a tear from her eye. "I imagined the whole thing, and I am nothin' but a liar."

She stood up, looking down to Imanie's grave, tears dripping down her cheeks. "Oh, Imanie, why are ye no' here for me when I need ye, like ye were for the others? My cousins and even my own sister dinna believe me about Mazelina. And I promised Bedivere I wouldna say anythin' about my uncles and faither's lives bein' in danger, or else they might have believed me. And now, my da doesna want me to marry Bedivere because he thinks the man is just an assassin. But I love him, Imanie. I want to help Bedivere because he has had to kill men he didna even ken in order to protect his family. I would do anythin' to help him, even die if I had to."

"Well, then it's your lucky day," came a voice from behind her.

Morag spun around on her heel to find Whitmore right behind her holding the hilt of his sword above her head.

"Nay!" she cried, holding up her hands to hide her face as the man's sword came right toward her.

CHAPTER 23

"So, you see, I think I can get Whitmore to confess to all of this. And with you three hiding in the brush to hear it, we'll be able to convict him." Bedivere stood in the stables staring at the bastard triplets who stared back at him, not saying a word.

He had just explained everything to them hoping, if nothing else, it would ease Reed's hatred toward him so he could still marry the man's daughter.

"This is quite a story," said Rowen, leaning against the gate of the stall, rolling a piece of straw in his fingers.

"And it's all made up," said Reed, still scowling at him over his shoulder. "The man is an assassin and he is no' goin' to marry Morag. I willna allow it."

"Calm down, Brother," said Rook, sitting on a wooden bench, shining an apple on his sleeve and taking a bite. "It could be true since we already know Whitmore has been scheming against King Richard."

"You said Whitmore wanted you to kill us?" asked Rowen,

throwing down the piece of straw and resting his hand on the hilt of his sword. "Why didn't you?"

"I told you, I refused to do it since I knew the three of you would never betray your own blood."

"We raided our own faither, ye fool," spat Reed. "Or did ye forget about that?"

Bedivere had left out the part that he'd saved both Rook and Rowen's lives. He also didn't tell them about the other two assassins. It might have helped his case to tell them but, then again, these men had pride. They weren't going to admit that they needed saving. That might only turn them against him in the end if they didn't want to look weak in anyone's eyes. Being saved by an assassin wasn't something men would boast about.

"How do you plan on saving your mother?" Rook stretched out his legs and took another bite of the apple."

"I'm not sure yet. I have a dilemma. If I kill Whitmore, his men have been ordered to kill my mother in return. And I don't see that they are going to let me walk into the dungeon and just take her with me. Then again, if I don't kill him, he'll keep my mother imprisoned forever to keep me from telling Richard what he's been doing these past two years."

"Let me get this straight," said Reed, turning and crossing his arms over his chest. "Ye were killin' off innocent men? Or were they truly plottin' against the king?"

"I'm . . . not really sure about that part. Yet," said Bedivere. "But I hope to get the truth out of Whitmore once I talk with him in the woods. Now, will you three come with me or not?"

"How do we know this isn't some kind of crazy plan to get us in the woods and kill us?" asked Rook suspiciously. "You could have a small army lying in wait and that's why you want us away from the castle." Rook threw the apple core over his shoulder, wiped his hands on his breeches and stood up. "Mayhap, Brothers, we should kill him now and not take the chance he's planned an ambush for us."

"I'm all for that." Reed drew his sword and took a step toward Bedivere, but Rowen's arm shot out to block him.

"Not so fast," commanded Rowen. "If Bedivere can get Whitmore to confess and we are witnesses, Richard will be very grateful to us."

"True," said Rook. "We were planning on approaching the king about Whitmore even though we knew he wouldn't believe us. This will prove to Richard that our intent is to help him and not harm him."

"Richard has never trusted us since we raided his grandfather," added Rowen.

"Will you do it?" asked Bedivere.

"Even if we agree, ye are still no' marryin' my daughter," Reed reminded him.

"Bedivere, are you in here?" Percival entered the stable and stopped when he saw his brother talking to all three of the Legendary Bastards. "Oh, I'm sorry. I didn't know you were busy."

"What is it, Percival?" asked Bedivere.

"I'm sorry to bother you, but I thought you might want to know that Uncle Theobald thought he saw Whitmore leaving the castle and heading toward the woods a half-hour ago. Although with his eyesight going, he couldn't be sure it was him so mayhap it is nothing."

"I know about it," said Bedivere. "I'm meeting him."

"Do you think it's safe?" asked Percival.

Bedivere raised his brows. "Brother, you do know my

profession," he reminded him. "And I'll have the Legendary Bastards of the Crown along with me. So unless Uncle Theobald saw him leave with a small army, I think we can take care of ourselves."

"Aye, I understand," said Percival. "But that's not what I meant. I just saw the Ladies Willow, Maira and Fia return to the castle and that young squire, Branton, told me they'd been to the woods."

"Were they in a wagon?" asked Rowen.

"Nay. On horseback," Percival told them.

"What were they doing out there?" asked Rook, sounding concerned. "My daughter is very pregnant and I don't want her atop a horse. I'll have her head!"

"Was Morag with them?" asked Bedivere, concerned for her safety.

"I didn't see her," said Percival.

"It's odd that the other girls would leave without her," said Rowen.

"Oh, no," said Bedivere, having a terrifying thought. "She wouldn't have!" He ran from the stable with the rest of the men right behind him. "Where is Morag?" he shouted to the girls, who were dismounted and handing the reins of their horses to Branton.

The girls looked at each other but didn't say a word.

"Fia, where is yer sister?" growled Reed. "And dinna lie to me. I need to ken."

"She was with us," said Fia. "But she wanted some time alone."

"She's in the secret garden," said Branton. "I was just about to go back to get her."

"God's eyes," spat Bedivere. "Whitmore just left for the

woods and Morag is out there all alone. I've got to protect her." He took the reins from one of the horses from Branton, getting atop the animal in one jump.

"I'll show you the way," offered Branton.

"I know the way," said Bedivere.

"Then I'll help you protect her, since this is my fault for leaving her there all alone."

"I'm coming with you." Rowen jumped atop another horse.

"I'm in as well," said Rook doing the same.

"Morag is my daughter and no one is goin' to save her but me. Where's another horse? I need a horse," shouted Reed.

Branton and Bedivere took off for the drawbridge and both Rowen and Rook looked down at their brother and then over to each other.

"Last one out the gate gets him," said Rowen, kicking his heels into his horse and hurrying away, leaving Rook there.

"Move over, Rook," said Reed, pulling himself atop the horse behind his brother.

"Why is it always me?" grumbled Rook, taking off after the rest of the men.

As soon as they approached the secret garden and found the gate open, Bedivere knew Whitmore was inside.

"Hold up." Bedivere held up his hand to stop the others. Dismounting quickly, he pulled a blade from his waist belt and snuck up to the gate, peering inside. Sure enough, there were two horses inside. Whitmore was mounting one with Morag already atop, her hands tied and a gag in her mouth.

"Good God, he's got Morag."

"Let us through. I am goin' to kill him." Reed, sitting behind Rook on the horse, urged him to move closer.

"Wait!" Bedivere held up a halting hand again.

"Dinna tell me to wait when my daughter's life is in peril because of ye," Reed answered. "Rook, go on in the garden and hurry."

"If we all storm in there, he is sure to kill her," said Bedivere. "Let me go in first and try to talk to him. We need to keep him calm and make him feel like he's got the upper hand. Let's not even tell him the rest of you are here."

"He's right," said Rowen. "If Whitmore feels threatened, he might harm Morag."

"Well, I am no' goin' to sit here like a fool while Morag's life is in danger!" Reed dismounted and pulled his sword from the sheath. Rook jumped off the horse and grabbed his brother's hand.

"Don't be a fool, Reed," Rook warned him. "Bedivere is our best bet to deal with Whitmore. If he sees us, then it's all over. Let him try."

Reed looked at his brothers, his jaw ticking in aggravation. Then he shook Rook's hand off his arm. "Fine. Do what ye have to, but I am goin' to sneak up to the other side and come up behind him. I'll give ye only a few minutes, and if ye canna get Morag from him, then I am goin' to attack him from behind."

"I'll not only save Morag, I'll get to him confess to everything," Bedivere promised. "So all of you, even you, Branton, stay close enough to hear every word he says, but keep hidden. Then, after Morag is safe, we take him back to the castle at the ends of our blades."

Bedivere slowly stepped into the secret garden, hoping to hell he could do everything he'd promised, ready to give his life to save Morag if need be.

* * *

MORAG'S HEAD felt like it was split open from the hit of the hilt of Whitmore's sword. She'd fallen to the ground, unconscious, and when she awoke, he had her hands tied and a gag in her mouth.

Sitting atop the man's horse, Morag felt dizzy and ready to retch. She didn't even have a dagger with her and now regretted telling the others to leave her behind. She had never expected Whitmore to show up here. And mayhap, if she hadn't been so focused on talking to a woman who was dead, she would have seen Whitmore enter the garden and sneak up behind her.

Morag feared for her life and felt like a fool. She needed to be strong, she told herself. Strong like Maira, Willow, and Fia. But she didn't feel strong at all. She felt like a frightened child who had made a big mistake and would pay for it with her life.

She couldn't even talk to Whitmore to beg him to let her go because she had a blasted gag in her mouth.

Funny, when one is about to die, the thoughts that go through one's head. She wondered how Bedivere's mother fared in the dungeon for two long years, where she slept, what she ate, and if she ever cried. Then she found herself thinking about Bedivere and how brave he'd been to make the deal to be an assassin to save each member of his family. How awful it must have felt every time he had to slit a man's throat. His actions would most likely haunt him for the rest of his life.

Aye, she now regretted not paying heed to Bedivere's orders about not being in the woods unescorted. She would even welcome the annoying Branton right now since he'd proven in the past he knew how to wield a sword, saving her from bandits along the road.

Her father was going to be so angry with her if she wound up dead. And Bedivere would most likely be blamed for it. She never even had the chance to explain to her father how much she loved Bedivere. Neither would her father ever know what Bedivere did, saving the lives of both her uncles.

"Now I have the leverage I need," chuckled Whitmore climbing atop the horse behind her. "Your lover will never deny my orders again, and neither will he ever reveal my secrets. Because if he does, my dear, you will die."

"Let her go, Whitmore."

Morag turned her head to see Bedivere enter the garden, holding his sword steady in two hands. "You hurt her and I'll personally sever your head from your body."

Whitmore pulled Morag closer to him, making her gasp. Then he took the edge of his dagger and pressed it against her throat. The steel felt cold and sharp and she didn't dare to even swallow for fear she'd move and send the blade into her throat.

"Bedivere, what took you so long?" asked Whitmore. "Now, shall we make that deal we talked about?"

"I'll never make a deal with you. Now let her go."

"I can't do that. You have become a burden to me, and I can no longer keep an assassin who refuses his orders."

"Take me instead," said Bedivere. "But just don't hurt Morag."

"I see how much she means to you. Now I have all the leverage I need."

Morag noticed Bedivere's eyes dart to one side of the garden and then the other. When she followed his gaze she saw her father hiding behind the stable. Her Uncle Rook crept over the porch of the cottage, staying in the shadows. If she looked hard enough, she thought she saw her Uncle Rowen behind a tree. And by a flash of brown from behind the garden gate, she recognized Branton's tunic.

"I know your game, Whitmore." Bedivere walked forward slowly, keeping his sword steady. "You advise Richard, but only to gain the lands and riches from the men you've had me kill."

"What difference does it make?" asked Whitmore.

"What do you think Richard will say when he finds out what you've been doing for the past two years?"

"He'll thank me for eliminating men who wanted to see his demise. He won't care that I took their holdings. The fact of the matter is that eleven times now, I've kept him from being assassinated."

"Then, you're saying those men I've killed really were plotting against the king?"

"Aye, of course they were."

"But what about my father? I'm sure he wouldn't do such a thing."

"Nay, your father was much too devoted to Richard to ever do a thing against him. Unfortunately, he was at the wrong place at the wrong time and overheard me talking to one of my contacts. He knew I'd planned to gain as much land and wealth as I could by advising the king I deserved it, after my assassins eliminated the threats against him."

"My father was going to turn you in to the king, wasn't he?" Bedivere moved in closer. Whitmore turned the horse slightly.

"Aye, your father, Sir Gilbert Hamilton, was much too

revered by Richard. He was also after my position as advisor to the king. If he had told Richard my plans, he would be the new advisor and I would have not only been removed, but most likely imprisoned and eventually killed. So you see, I couldn't allow him to do that."

"So you made up the false charge that he was plotting against Richard."

"Aye, and it worked like a charm. But you were too much a devoted son and gave me trouble. That's why I decided to take you as well as your family into custody for added insurance."

"You are naught but a spawn of the devil!" shouted Bedivere. Morag saw his face become red and anger glaring in his eyes. "You killed my father, an innocent man, and put my family, even the children through a living hell."

"Aye. And if you hadn't brought your family to Rothbury, they would be back in the dungeon right now and you would be working for me for the rest of your life."

"That, I promise you, will never happen."

"Mayhap not, but if you ever want to see your mother as well as your lover alive again, you'll keep quiet and continue doing my bidding."

"Nay, he won't, because we've just heard enough to put you behind bars forever, Whitmore." Rowen stepped out from behind a tree, and Rook and Reed made their presence known as well.

"You knew we were on to you and that is why you wanted Bedivere to kill us, isn't that right?" asked Rook, coming closer. Each of the men held their swords out, ready to fight.

"It would have worked, too, if Bedivere hadn't stopped my assassins from killing you." Whitmore's arm tightened around Morag as he suddenly became very nervous.

"Wait. What?" asked Rook. "Bedivere saved our lives?"

"That's right," said Bedivere. "Rook, I took out the assassin that was planning on killing you during the joust and impersonated him on the field. I then pretended to be injured by the lance when, in fact, it was from the assassin's blade."

"I'm willing to bet that healer was an assassin as well," said Rowen. "He certainly didn't seem to know a thing about herbs or ointments."

"He tried to poison you," Bedivere told him. "So I took care of him as well."

"Impressive." Rowen and Rook nodded at each other.

"Enough talk! Ye have my daughter and I'll no' wait a minute longer." When Reed rushed forward, Morag reached upward. Even with her hands tied together, she managed to push the blade away from her throat.

"You fool! He could have killed her," shouted Bedivere as Whitmore turned the horse and took off at a run for the gate. Morag bounced up and down as they rode, managing to reach up and yank the gag from her mouth.

As they left the garden, Branton stepped out with his sword drawn, startling the horse. Whitmore's steed reared up, and Morag grabbed on to the animal's mane to keep from being thrown.

"Morag, hold on, I'm coming!" shouted Bedivere as Whitmore directed the horse away from the garden at a run. She heard the thundering hooves of a horse from behind them, and looked back to see Bedivere atop his horse in fast pursuit.

"If I'm going to die, then I'm taking you with me," Whitmore said in her ear. As they rode, he pressed his blade once again against her throat, and this time she felt the sting of the sharp metal and the blood trickling down her neck. She reached up, struggling with Whitmore, trying to keep away from his blade. Bedivere rode up next to them as they shot through the forest at high speed.

"Jump!" Bedivere called to her, holding his sword and reins in one hand and reaching out for her.

"Jump?" Morag eyed the trees whizzing past them so fast that it made her head spin. Too frightened to do it, she froze in fear. "I canna."

"Trust me," he shouted. "I'll catch you. Jump now, before it's too late."

Suddenly hearing Mazelina's voice in her head telling her to be brave and to do something to make a difference in the world, Morag realized she had to try. Then, with her hands still tied in front of her, and the horses running faster than she could imagine, she focused on Bedivere and not the ground speeding by as she took a leap of faith.

Morag flung her body toward Bedivere and his arm shot out and clasped around her wrist as she landed hard on her stomach atop his lap.

"I've got you, Morag," he said, still in pursuit of Whitmore. He helped her up to a sitting position, pulling a dagger from his belt and swiping at the ropes that bound her hands. "Hold on to the horse's mane," he instructed. "And don't watch what I'm about to do because this isn't going to be pretty."

She was about to ask him what he meant, when Bedivere rode up next to Whitmore and, with one blow of his sword, decapitated the man. Morag, being too curious as always and never any good at following instructions, had watched and now she wished that she hadn't.

Turning her head, she vomited over the side of the horse.

As soon as Bedivere stopped the horse, her father, uncles, and Branton rode up.

"Thank God ye killed him," said Reed, hopping off his horse and inspecting Whitmore's body. "If ye hadna done it, I would have. Morag, are ye all right?"

"Aye, Da. Bedivere saved my life." Emotions welled in Morag. After Bedivere helped her from the horse, she hugged and kissed him, never wanting to let him go.

She looked up to see her father standing there, looking at her with sadness in his eyes.

"Morag, go to your father," Bedivere whispered, kissing her atop the head and lightly pushing her toward Reed.

"Da?" Morag's lip quivered and she burst into tears. Her father dropped his sword and held out his arms and Morag ran to him and buried her head against his chest. "Da, I am so sorry for makin' ye angry with me. I only wanted ye to love me the same way ye love Fia."

Reed dropped to his knees, holding on to Morag and they continued to hug.

"Morag," he said, holding her tightly to his chest and rubbing his cheek against her head. She felt his body shaking and noticed a tear dripping down his cheek that wasn't hers. "I have never been so frightened in my life. I thought I had lost ye. Dinna ever think I dinna love ye because that is the furthest thing from the truth."

"But ye always seem to forget me and I didna think ye were proud of me since I canna do the things that Fia does."

"I love ye in a whole different way than Fia, but that doesna mean I love ye less."

Morag then looked into her father's eyes and talked from

her heart. "Da, I love Bedivere and I want to be his wife. Please, will ye agree to the marriage?"

Reed stood up, bringing Morag with him. Rowen, Rook, and Branton watched on.

"Do ye love Morag?" Reed asked Bedivere after releasing a deep breath.

Bedivere walked up to them and got down on one knee, taking Morag's hand in his. He looked into her eyes as he spoke.

"I love your daughter," Bedivere told Reed. "More than life itself."

Morag smiled, feeling her heart swell. Everything was going to be all right now. She was sure of it.

"Ye saved Morag's life," said Reed. "I can never repay ye. If ye want to marry my daughter . . . then I agree to it."

Morag barely felt the pain in her body anymore because she was so happy that she could burst. Finally, she would get what she always wanted. She would marry Bedivere and they would have a family. She had found the love she always longed for in her heart.

"I love you, Morag," Bedivere told her. "But I am sorry, I cannot marry you after all."

CHAPTER 24

"What did ye say?" Morag blinked away the tears as Bedivere stood up and dropped her hand.

"I am not good enough for you," said Bedivere. "You certainly deserve someone other than an assassin for your husband."

"B-but I want ye, Bedivere. Ye are no' an assassin. Ye did those things to save yer family."

"Morag, I want you more than you know." Bedivere looked back to Whitmore's body lying on the ground. "However, I let my anger take hold of me. I just killed a man who didn't need to die."

"I'm no' so sure I agree with that," said Reed.

"How do you think King Richard is going to react to someone murdering his advisor?" asked Branton.

"It wasna murder, Branton," said Morag. "Bedivere did it to save me."

"We'll do what we can to help by telling the king the truth," said Rowen.

"Aye, mayhap that will help his verdict." Bedivere didn't sound as if he believed it.

"Verdict? What do ye mean?" asked Morag.

"He might be sentenced to death for this," said Branton.

"Nay." Morag shook her head. "Richard wouldna do that."

"Hopefully not," said Rook. "After all, we can attest to the fact that Bedivere stopped eleven men who were plotting against him."

"If he listens to us," said Reed. "Richard never liked us and ye all ken it."

"If he doesna listen to ye then mayhap he'll listen to me. After all, I am his cousin," Morag reminded them.

"Nay, Morag. Don't get involved," begged Bedivere. "This is my battle, not yours. If Richard won't pardon me, you don't need him to be angry with you as well."

"Bedivere Hamilton, for bein' such a brave man, sometimes ye can act so stupid," remarked Morag.

"Stupid?" Bedivere shook his head. "Don't you realize I am trying to save you from being a young widow if the king orders my execution? Morag, I am only trying to protect you and keep you from being hurt."

"Execution? Nay, Richard wouldna do that. Would he, Da?"

"I'm no' sure, Morag," answered Reed softly. "I guess we'll have to wait and see what happens."

"Well, I dinna care." Morag lifted her chin and looked everyone there in the eye.

"You don't care what happens to me?" Bedivere sounded very disappointed.

"That's no' what I mean." Morag felt confident for the first time in her life. "What I mean is that I dinna care what happens to me. I love ye, Bedivere and I want to marry ye now, and no' wait. No matter what the consequences of yer actions."

"Morag, think what you're saying." Bedivere took her hands in his. "If I am convicted and sentenced to die for my past ways, I don't want my wife to have to watch that."

"I would be there no matter if I am yer wife or no' so stop tryin' to protect me because ye are only hurtin' me instead."

"Do you really feel that way?" asked Bedivere.

"I do."

"And knowing what I did and the demons in my head that will be haunting me for the rest of my life, not to mention all the wagging tongues – you still want me as your husband?"

"Because of those demons that might haunt ye, and all the waggin' tongues, I want to be at yer side even more. I will be there every step of the way to help ye get through this."

"Oh, Morag, I love you." He pulled her into his arms. "And like I said, I don't deserve you. But if you still want me, and your father agrees to the marriage, then I don't see why we shouldn't be wed."

"Da?" Morag asked, looking up to her father who was no longer frowning, but smiling instead. "Did ye mean it when ye said ye agreed to our marriage?"

"Agree to it?" he asked. "I'll no' only agree, but I'll shout it from the rooftops because I am proud of both of ye. Aye, Sir Bedivere, ye have my permission to marry my daughter, Morag. I'd like to welcome ye, even though ye are a Sassenach, into our family."

"Morag," said Bedivere. "If you don't mind, I'd like to do one more thing before we get married."

"Clean up the mess?" Morag couldn't even look at Whitmore's body.

"Besides that," Bedivere answered. "I'd like to free my mother and bring her back to Rothbury for our wedding."

"Can ye do that?" asked Morag. "Will Whitmore's men even let ye near the dungeon? And once they find out ye killed Whitmore, will they come after ye instead?"

"I don't know but it's a chance I'll have to take. Please understand, my mother has been imprisoned for two long years and I can't stand to think of her locked away in that horrible place, not even for another minute."

"Then do it," said Morag. "And when ye get back, we will have the best weddin' there ever was. I will tell Lady Ernestine that the weddin' is on again."

Rook, Reed, and Rowen mumbled to each other and then Reed spoke up. "We're comin' with ye, Bedivere. And if anyone there gives ye a hard time about springin' yer mathair from the dungeon, they are goin' to have to take on the rest of yer family."

"My family?" asked Bedivere.

"Aye, yer family," said Reed, nodding to his brothers. "Well, what are we waitin' for? We've got a lot to do and I suggest we get movin.'"

"Thank ye, Da," said Morag, reaching out and hugging her father with one arm while she hugged Bedivere with the other.

CHAPTER 25

Morag paced back and forth nervously in her chamber, not having slept at all since Bedivere, her father, and her uncles left for Whitmore Castle. It had been over two days now and, still, they hadn't returned.

"Morag, hurry," said Fia. "Everyone is already in the courtyard."

"Aye," added Willow. "Lady Ernestine has announced that she's made her decision."

"I dinna care to go," said Morag. "I'm afeared somethin' has happened to Bedivere and our faithers. Why are none of ye worried?"

"Morag, ye dinna need to worry about Da or Uncle Rowen and Uncle Rook." Fia wrapped her baby up in a blanket as she spoke.

"That's true," added Maira. "They are the Legendary Bastards of the Crown and have been through a lot worse than this."

"I suppose," said Morag. "But I am concerned for Bedivere

as well. I love him so much that I dinna ken what I'd do if somethin' happened to him."

"He'll be back soon," Fia told her. "And then ye two will be married. Now come on, Morag. We're goin' to miss all the excitement." Fia picked up the baby and she and Maira headed out the door. Willow followed, but stopped at the threshold and looked back.

"Are you coming?" asked Willow.

Morag stared out the window and sighed. "I suppose so." With her head down, she made her way to the door.

"Wait, Morag." Willow stopped her from leaving. "There is something I want to say to you first."

"What is it, Cousin?"

"It's about Bedivere. I'm sorry for what I said about him. I am afraid I haven't been too kind to him or even to you. However, I have a much different opinion of him now that I know his story."

"It's all right," said Morag softly.

"I also want to be honest with you and tell you that, at one time, Bedivere kissed me and wanted to marry me."

"I ken that."

"Aye, but what you don't know is that he said even though it didn't work out, he still wanted to marry someone like me."

"I see," said Morag, feeling a little disappointed. "I suppose men always dream of marryin' someone like ye, Willow. But I've changed. I think. I am tryin' no' to be such a gossip anymore."

"Morag, what I meant is that he's getting someone better than me." Willow smiled and put her arm around Morag's shoulders. "You two are a perfect couple and I am sure you will be very happy together."

"Do ye think everythin' is all right, Willow? I canna help but worry that somethin' went wrong since they are no' back yet."

"Everything will be just fine, I promise you."

"But how do ye ken?"

"I know because I feel it in here." Willow laid a hand over her heart. "We are Followers of the Secret Heart, Morag. We know these things because we listen to our hearts. Listen to yours and it will tell you the same thing."

"I dinna ken how."

"Here. Let me help you." Willow took Morag's hand and placed it over her heart. "Close your eyes," she said. "Close your eyes and think of Bedivere and you will know that everything is going to be fine."

Morag closed her eyes and pictured Bedivere standing before her, smiling. He had his mother with him. "I feel it. I see it," she said excitedly. "Ye are right. I can listen to my heart and know the truth."

"Morag?"

Morag opened her eyes to see Bedivere poking his head into the room. "What are you doing?"

"Bedivere!" Morag ran to him and fell into his arms, kissing and hugging him because she was so happy to see him safe and alive. Then she noticed the gaunt, pale woman standing next to him. Her eyes had dark circles under them and she was naught but skin and bones. However, she was smiling.

"Morag, I'd like you to meet my mother, Lady Ada."

"Oh, Bedivere, ye were able to save her!" Morag said excitedly. "Lady Ada, I am so happy to meet ye."

"Nay," said the woman, "it is me who is happy to meet the

lady my son tells me was the one who kept him from giving up. I am happy that you will be his wife."

"What happened in Whitmore?" asked Morag. "Why did it take ye so long?"

"So long?" asked Bedivere. "Morag, we rode day and night and didn't even sleep, just to make it back here as fast as possible. Plus, we met someone on the road just as we approached the castle."

"Who?" asked Morag.

All of a sudden, Morag heard the straight trumpets announcing someone and, by the fanfare, she knew it was more than just a knight or a baron. She ran to the window and looked out to see the royal entourage of the king entering the courtyard.

"Richard is here?"

"Aye," said Bedivere. "He was on his way here for the choosing of the earl's holdings and we ran into him."

"Does he ken?"

"He knows everything," said Bedivere. "And just to ease your mind, he has pardoned not only me, but also my deceased father. He has cleared our family name. I will no longer have to feel shame."

"Richard used to be a good friend of my husband," said Ada. "He knew that Gilbert would never plot against him. Actually, he was the one who sent Gilbert as a spy to find out who his enemies were. When he heard what happened, he was understanding. Plus, he thanked Bedivere personally after Lord Rook and Lord Rowen told him how he'd saved their lives."

"So everythin' is all right now?" asked Morag.

"Aye, and my family as well as the priest, the king, and

everyone else are down in the courtyard waiting for us to get married."

"Married? Now?" Morag's heart sped up. She had been so preoccupied thinking about Bedivere that she had almost forgotten that as soon as he returned they were to be married.

"Hurry up and dress for the wedding, Morag," said Bedivere.

"I am dressed."

"Morag!" Willow shook her head. "You can't go to your wedding wearing that."

"But these are my clothes and I dinna have anythin' fancy."

"Well, then it's a good thing I have something for you to wear." Willow held out her hand to Lady Ada. "Lady Ada, if you wouldn't mind, I'd like to dress you for your son's wedding as well."

"Me?" Lady Ada looked up in surprise. The clothes she wore were naught but rags and very dirty.

"Go on, Mother." Bedivere nodded. "I'll meet all of you down in the courtyard, but hurry."

Bedivere left and closed the door, leaving Willow, Lady Ada, and Morag standing there looking at each other.

"You are pregnant," said Lady Ada, seeing Willow's large belly. "Congratulations."

"Thank you," said Willow heading over to her trunk and lifting the lid. "Come, try on your gown, Morag."

"Willow, I do no' think I'll fit into anythin' of yers."

Willow held up a blue gown with long, trailing tippets make of silk and lace.

"Of course not, silly. I am six month's pregnant. But you will fit in this gown that Maira, Fia, and I made for you out of one of Maira's dresses."

"Ye mean, they made it," Morag corrected her.

"Nay, I mean all of us did. Actually, I was the one to do most of the sewing."

Morag giggled and rolled her eyes. "Now, that is a made up story if I ever heard one. Willow, it's no secret that ye dinna ken how to sew."

"I do now." Willow handed Morag the gown and picked up a small baby's dress, holding it in the air. "I learned, and have been sewing clothes for my baby."

"Do you think you are having a girl?" asked Ada.

"I am not sure. And that is why I made this as well." Willow proudly displayed an outfit for a little boy, too. "And Morag, as soon as you are pregnant, I will make clothes for your children as well."

"This is beautiful," said Morag, holding up the gown in front of her. "Willow, marriage sure has changed ye."

"Marriage will change you, too. Hopefully, for the better," added Willow with a giggle.

"What about a gown for Lady Ada?" asked Morag.

"Oh, no, that's all right," said Ada. "I have lost so much weight being imprisoned that I am sure none of those gowns are going to fit me."

"Then we'll do something about that." Willow picked up a small box and pulled out a needle and thread. "Lady Ada, would you like your gown to be yellow, orange, or burgundy?"

Morag watched as Lady Ada's eyes lit up and she went over to the trunk to choose a gown. Sometimes, the little things in life were taken for granted. Morag knew that now. Something as simple as a gown seemed to make Lady Ada come back to life. Morag felt blessed at this very moment and knew that she would never take anyone or anything for granted again.

A HALF-HOUR LATER, Morag walked through archways that were brightly decorated with colorful ribbons and bows. She wore her new gown and clutched a bouquet of fresh, small, white flowers that Maira and Fia had picked for her from down by the creek. Lady Ada had woven spring violets of purple and blue into Morag's braid making her feel like a queen.

Morag didn't have a fancy crown like her sister or cousins, but she no longer needed one, she decided. She was marrying Sir Bedivere, and that was more than she could ever ask for.

She made her way through the very crowded courtyard with Fia, Maira, and Willow all walking with her, arm in arm. She'd insisted on it, since this was her special day and they were her family.

When they got to the dais, she saw her cousin, King Richard, sitting with Lady Ernestine. He nodded to her and she nodded back. Now, she felt even more special than the other girls since she had a king at her wedding, not to mention a good amount of nobility from across the land.

"Morag, you are beautiful." Bedivere stood at the foot of the dais by the priest, holding on to the arm of his mother. Lady Ada looked beautiful and so happy now that she was cleaned up. She had chosen a bright yellow gown. Bedivere gave his mother a kiss on the head and escorted her over to sit with his aunt, uncle, and siblings.

Morag's family sat on the other side. When she got to the

front, Willow took her flowers and the girls stood off to the side.

The priest walked forward with his prayer book in his hand. "This is a very special wedding with two amazing people," said the priest before he proceeded to marry them. When Bedivere placed a ring on Morag's finger, she looked up to him in surprise.

"Where did ye get this?" she asked.

"It was my mother's wedding ring," he told her. "She said she wanted you to have it."

Morag felt the tears in her eyes. This was the last memory the woman had left of her late husband and she gave it to Morag even though she barely knew her. After the vows, they kissed and everyone clapped and cheered. Then King Richard stood, and the crowd silenced.

"I, King Richard, would like to be the first to congratulate my cousin, Morag, on her marriage to Sir Bedivere."

The crowd cheered once again, the sound of the roar sent an exciting shiver up Morag's spine. She had never felt so important and noticed in all her life. Everyone was paying attention to her and she loved it.

Next, Lady Ernestine stood up. Once again, the crowd silenced. The king continued.

"Lady Rothbury has been surveying every knight, baron, and earl on the list for the past two weeks and has finally come to a conclusion."

Everyone listened intently as they waited for their name to be called.

"I asked her to give me three names of the men she thought were the most worthy of inheriting the late earl's holdings," continued Richard. "However, she has only given me one."

Now, the crowd seemed to get upset. A low mumble of voices filled the courtyard.

"I have spoken with her, and decided that there is no need for more than one name, because only one man deserves to inherit the earl's castle, lands, and riches."

"Who is it?" someone called out anxiously.

King Richard nodded to Lady Ernestine. "I will let the Lady of Rothbury tell us who she has chosen."

Lady Ernestine stepped forward and looked out at the crowd. "It is my pleasure to announce that the man who will inherit my late husband's holdings is a very brave man. He thinks of others before himself and has saved not only my life, but the life of the king, as well as Lady Morag. Congratulations, Sir Bedivere Hamilton, the late earl's estate is all yours."

"Me?" Bedivere's eyes opened wide in surprise, but the crowd remained silent.

Morag's heart stilled. She felt as if the people didn't accept him, and she wondered if they all knew his secret.

Then Reed stood up and slowly started clapping. Rook and Rowen jumped up and did the same. Before she knew it, everyone was on their feet applauding and congratulating not only Bedivere but also Morag.

"Bedivere, I canna believe this," she said shyly, looking out to the crowd in awe.

Bedivere leaned closer and spoke in her ear. "Morag, because of your father's help, as well as the words to the king from your uncles, I am cleared of all charges. Richard has thanked me for saving him from the men who had conspired against him. He was a little disappointed that I'd killed Whitmore, but only because he wanted the pleasure of doing it himself."

"Throw the bouquet," called out someone from the crowd.

"Here, Morag." Willow placed the flowers in Morag's hands.

"Oh, all right," she said, closing her eyes and tossing the bouquet out to the crowd.

Everyone started laughing and she didn't know why. When she opened her eyes, Branton held the flowers and had an odd look on his face.

"Why do I always end up with this?" asked Branton.

"Well, Squire," yelled out Maira's husband, Sir Jacob. "Mayhap, it is time for you to get married."

"Nay," said Branton, taking the bouquet and hurriedly handing it to Lady Ada.

"I love you, Morag," said Bedivere. "And I want to thank you for saying you'd always be at my side to help me through any rough times I might have from the demons of my past."

"I love ye, too," said Morag, kissing her new husband. "And I want ye to ken that this is the happiest day of my life."

EPILOGUE

ONE YEAR LATER

*M*orag held her new baby girl, Mazelina, in her arms as she and her sister and cousins paid a visit to the secret garden.

Fia was pregnant again, and held the hand of her daughter, Oletha. She helped the little girl to sniff all the beautiful flowers that made the garden come to life and seem so magical once again. Maira had a daughter named Sable and Willow's nine-month-old girl was Siusan.

Willow's sister by marriage, Hazel, and another Follower of the Secret Heart, Sister Adeline, were there visiting as well.

"Hazel, you and Morag have done wonders with this garden," said Willow, picking up her daughter who was crawling in the dirt.

"Hazel always did have a magical touch when it came to gardenin'," said Morag. "And when I'm often back in Scotland

239

visitin' with my family, she and Sister Adeline keep the flowers watered and the weeds pulled."

"It looks amazin'," said Fia, picking a flower and giving it to her daughter.

"Tell me, Morag," said Sister Adeline, fixing her wimple. "What made you decide to name your daughter, Mazelina?"

"She named it after the woman who supposedly mentored her," said Maira.

"Mazelina did mentor me," scoffed Morag, never having been able to convince her sister and cousins that she had really seen the woman.

"I've only heard that name once before," said Sister Adeline. "It was the name of Imanie's sister."

"Ye ken her?" asked Morag, very excited. Now, perhaps, someone would believe her.

"Oh, I never met her personally," replied the nun. "But Imanie mentioned her from time to time. It seems Imanie made her sister a member of the Followers of the Secret Heart, right before Mazelina mysteriously died."

"Died?" Morag couldn't believe it. "Nay, she's still alive. I talked to her. She mentored me."

"Mayhap ye dreamed it," said Maira. "After all, the three of us saw Imanie in our dreams many times and still talked to her that way."

"I'm sorry, Morag, but it couldn't be her you speak of," said Sister Adeline. "After all, you couldn't have ever even known her. She died years before you girls came to live at Rothbury."

Morag didn't want to hear this, because it was only going to make things worse for her. Now, her sister and cousins would never believe her.

"Oletha, catch the ball," said Maira, tossing a ball to Fia's daughter, but the girl was young and couldn't catch. The ball rolled off into the bushes.

"I'll get it," said Morag. "Sister Adeline, will ye hold my baby?"

"I would love to," said the nun, taking the baby in her arms. Hazel walked up and they both smiled at the child and talked gibberish to her.

Disheartened to hear that she must have imagined being mentored by Mazelina, Morag pushed aside the bushes to get the ball. That's when she saw something in the dirt that didn't belong there.

"My heart brooch! I found it," Morag called to the others. When she looked back down to the ground she saw something else she had never noticed before. Under the thick shrubs was a broken wooden cross, lying on the earth. She picked up the cross and wiped off the dirt, seeing something etched into the wood. "Fia, Willow, Maira, come here quickly."

"What is it?" called out Fia. The girls left the children with Hazel and Sister Adeline and came to see what Morag wanted.

"Look!" Morag held out the wooden cross that had the name Mazelina scratched into it. "Imanie must have buried her sister here under the bush. And I have a feelin' she was the one Imanie told us that died after she made her a member."

"I think ye're right," said Fia.

When Morag looked back over her shoulder, she gasped. In the shadows of the garden behind the bush stood not only Mazelina but also Imanie.

"Please tell me the rest of ye see what I see," said Morag softly, hoping now the girls would believe her.

"What do you mean?" asked Maira.

"It is Imanie and Mazelina," Morag told them. She pointed to the bush. "They are standin' right there."

"I don't see anything but trees and flowers," said Willow.

"Neither do I," added Maira. She and Willow exchanged glances and then headed back to the children leaving only Fia there with her.

"Fia? Ye believe me, dinna ye?" Morag asked her sister.

Fia put her hand on Morag's shoulder, giving her a sympathetic smile. "Dinna let it bother ye, Morag, that we dinna see what ye do. If ye believe it . . . then I do, too." She gave her sister a hug and headed over to join the other girls.

"But they are really there," Morag cried to Fia's back, feeling frustrated and confused. When she looked back to where she saw Imanie and Mazelina, sadly, they were now gone. Holding the brooch tightly in her hand, she closed her eyes, missing the mentors. Then she heard Mazelina's voice in her head.

"Be strong, Morag," said Mazelina.

"But it is so hard. They dinna believe me," whispered Morag, feeling like crying. "I dinna ken how to make them see ye as well."

"They cannot see us," said Imanie. "That is your special gift alone."

"It is?" asked Morag, the words making her feel choked with emotion. "But I still wish they would believe me."

"Is it really that important to you? Do you need others' approval?" asked Mazelina.

Morag thought about it for a second and then realized that she didn't. "Nay," she answered. "I suppose I dinna need approval from anyone anymore," she said with a smile, feeling confident now that no one could rattle her nerves.

"You are a strong woman, Morag, and have proven it," said Imanie. "You deserve to wear the heart brooch."

"Aye," agreed Mazelina. "Do you feel now that you have truly earned your place as a Follower of the Secret Heart?"

"I do," Morag answered assuredly.

"We are proud of all four of you girls," Imanie told her. "You have proven to do wonderful things and so will your daughters someday."

"They will?" asked Morag excitedly. "Will they be Followers of the Secret Heart as well?"

Mazelina answered with a question as always. "Do you believe your daughters need to have a heart brooch and be members of a secret group to be strong women who do marvelous things in life?"

"Nay, I dinna think they do." Morag knew now that it didn't matter if the secret group ceased to exist. There would always be strong women in life, and no one had to appoint them to that position. "I believe we all have the ability to be strong and make a difference in the world. No one has to tell us what we are capable of doin' because all we need to do is feel it in our hearts to ken it is true."

"I think our job is done here now," Imanie told her sister.

"Nay, dinna leave," Morag begged them. "I will miss ye and dinna want to ever forget either of ye."

"Do you feel you need a mentor anymore, Morag?" asked Mazelina.

"I suppose no," said Morag. "Mayhap, it is time that my cousins and sister and I take the place of mentors to our daughters instead."

"Then we'll be going," said Imanie.

"Guidbye," Morag told them with a smile, feeling their

presence in her heart. "This garden will always be here, I'll make certain of that," she told them. "It will never be neglected again. It'll live on in the memory of both of ye. And someday, years from now, we will tell our daughters about no' only ye two, but also our experiences, and everythin' we've learned. They will be strong women just like us. And together, we will teach them, and tell them all about the *Forgotten Secrets*."

FROM THE AUTHOR

As the *Secrets of the Heart Series* comes to a close, I feel emotional, like I was a part of Fia, Willow, Maira, and Morag's journeys to becoming strong women.

We all have the ability within us to make a difference in the world and bring about positive changes. Confidence and believing in oneself is just the start of the journey. What we do with the skills and talents we have is up to us.

If you have missed any of the books in the series, I have listed them all for you. Be sure to also read about the girls' fathers in the *Legendary Bastards of the Crown Series*, and their aunts in the *Seasons of Fortitude Series*.

Remember to let love guide you on your journey and always be true to your heart.

Elizabeth

Secrets of the Heart Series:

Highland Secrets – Book 1
Seductive Secrets – Book 2
Rebellious Secrets – Book 3
Forgotten Secrets – Book 4

Legendary Bastards of the Crown:
Destiny's Kiss – Series Prequel
Restless Sea Lord – Book 1
Ruthless Knight – Book 2
Reckless Highlander – Book 3

Seasons of Fortitude Series:
Highland Spring – Book 1
Summer's Reign – Book 2
Autumn's Touch – Book 3
Winter's Flame – Book 4

ABOUT ELIZABETH

Elizabeth Rose is a multi-published, bestselling author, writing medieval, historical, contemporary, paranormal, and western romance. Her books are available as EBooks, paperbacks, and audiobooks as well.

Her favorite characters in her works include dark, dangerous and tortured heroes, and feisty, independent heroines who know how to wield a sword. She loves writing 14th century medieval novels, and is well-known for her many series.

Her twelve-book small town contemporary series, Tarnished Saints, was inspired by incidents in her own life.

After being traditionally published, she started self-publishing, creating her own covers and book trailers on a dare from her two sons.

Elizabeth loves the outdoors. In the summertime, you can find her in her secret garden with her laptop, swinging in her hammock working on her next book. Elizabeth is a born storyteller and passionate about sharing her works with her readers.

Please visit her website at **Elizabethrosenovels.com** to read excerpts from any of her novels and get sneak peeks at covers of upcoming books. You can follow her on **Twitter, Facebook**, **Goodreads** or **BookBub.** Be sure to sign up for her

newsletter so you don't miss out on new releases or upcoming events.

Cowboys of the Old West Series

And more!

Please visit http://elizabethrosenovels.com

Elizabeth Rose

Made in the USA
Middletown, DE
28 September 2021